She,
He, Them:
Full Circle

By

Karen D. Neal

This book was printed in the United States of America.

Credits

Editor/Cover Designer: Cassandra Sims

ACKNOWLEDGEMENTS

I am sitting here thanking God almighty for the endurance He constantly gives me. Without Him, there is no me. My dedication is short, for I have one person to thank, other than God, for finishing this book. This young lady and I wrote my first book together and I say that in all honesty. She encouraged me till the end with my first book, and often, she was my only support. Somewhere along the way, we parted ways for a couple of years, but God stepped in and steered us back together. I guess He knew I would never finish this book without her pushing me. Thank you, Cassandra Barrett Sims, for seeing in me what I don't see in myself.

FOREWORDS

This book is awesome. Lady you are Blessed in so many ways. When I started reading it I couldn't put it down. I finally finished She He Them: Full Circle. The shocker to me as I read your editors notes is that I take medication for Anxiety and I have panic attacks but I never put my excessive worrying and tension to be associated with my anxiety. Your book has really opened up my eyes and been a blessing to me to let me know that the other disorders I have could be related to my anxiety. Thank you for opening my eyes to mental issues and helping me realize that having a condition doesn't mean you are crazy. It's the blows that you were dealt in life that you depress. ~~~~Brenda Grissom

Karen D. Neal

This book is so informative of multiple personalities. It made me wonder if people with this disorder attract other people with the same disorder? The characters really came to life and showed how they have issues that we see in everyday life. Some people have more issues than others, and labels are placed on them by society, but the characters in this book proved, you don't have to keep that mindset. These are successful adults, who were condemned by society at young ages, but now finding love and getting second chances to get their lives right. ~~~Shelia Reeves

PROLOGUE

The room was dark except for the dimming lights that, ironically, only seemed to make it darker. The piercing beeping sounds coming from the monitors pecked at my nerves, creating an anxiety deep within, waiting to explode inside my body.

I sat beside the window refusing to take my eyes off of the bed. I saw very little proof of life in the body that lay there. I'd lost all sense of time and I couldn't even remember what day of the week it was. Any interests I once had for life was now gone, and I was focused on one thing, and one thing only. I was not leaving this place as long as the shallowest breath of life remained inside her. The explosive drama that occurred three days prior was a vision I couldn't seem to get out of my head.

A nurse entered the room and turned on the lights over the bed. My eyes remained fixated on the bed and I noticed her body move slightly— the first real proof of life I'd seen thus far. The nurse proceeded to check her vitals, simultaneously, scribbling notes on the hand-held chart.

As I continued my visual observation, the robust lady finished recording her hourly results and looked over in my direction. "Sir, I realize you hate to leave but you really need to get some rest, or you'll have no strength left to care for yourself. You need to stay healthy so if by chance she pulls through, you'll be strong enough to care for her. I'm almost certain she'll be ordered rehabilitation for at least six to eight weeks to regain her strength," she informed me before momentarily pausing. "Even if she pulls through, the two of you will have a long journey ahead of you," she added, adamantly. At her last statement, I turned my attention in her direction for the first time since she'd entered the room. "My face will be the first face she sees when she wakes," I said, without blinking an eye. "I'm not going anywhere," I added, in a stern yet calm tone. The nurse gave me a sympathetic smile as she walked out of the room.

STEPHINE

Stephine returned to the nurse's station shaking her head, pitifully. Dorinda, a pretty, petite nurse standing at best four feet and eleven inches tall, glanced up and noticed the look on her co-worker's face.

"Girl, what's got you lookin' so sour?" Dorinda asked with a matched expression of her own.

"The patient in room 211 has little to no chance of surviving, but her husband refuses to leave her side. I feel so sorry for him." Stephine continued shaking her head from side to side.

"Well, just because the prognosis looks bad doesn't mean it's too late for a miracle to happen," Dorinda stated with crossed arms, concerned about Stephine getting too personal in this case. Their motto was, "Feel empathy, never feel sympathy."

"I know you're right, but he just looks so beaten down, and girl, he is too damn fine to be wasting away, worrying about situations he has no control of," Stephine replied in defense of her feelings, while mockingly fanning her face. She looked at Dorinda with a matter-of-fact look, as she took a seat behind the desk. "Humph, I can help him with that grief process," she laughed, and winked flirtatiously.

Dorinda smiled and shook her head at her co-worker's humor. She knew Stephine was harmless and just full of talk, but she hoped her mouth wouldn't get her in trouble one day.

The ladies were busy with their individual tasks when the monitor in room 211 went off and the scanner started going crazy. Paper flew everywhere then they heard a loud crash come from the same room. They looked at one another, curiously, before jumping up, running towards the room.

Before they could make it to their destination, the hallway was swarmed with every medical attendant on the floor— all rushing to room 211. Stephine was the first to enter the room but she came to a screeching halt at what she saw before her eyes.

TONYA

It was day three in the holding cell and Tonya was four to five-seconds away from putting her foot in some girl's ass. The chick had been in her space five minutes too long trying hard to push her buttons.

"Yeah… look at you sittin' over there like you all that," the girl said. "But you doin' the right thing by keepin' your mouth shut 'cause I'm not the one you wanna be messin' with," she said in a provocative tone.

Tonya ignored the butch-looking young woman, but she was struggling internally as the chatter from the overcrowded cell echoed off the four small walls. Not that it was much better, but she was waiting for her daily reprieve from the madness. Besides, at least she'd only have two people to look at, versus looking at an over-crowded cell of women.

What's taking Officer Montauk so long to come get me? she thought. *I know he's coming because I've been getting interrogated every day since I got here. How many times am I going to have to re-live that damn day?* The voices began invading her mind and she was having a hell of a time keeping Mystik's dark side hidden. In fact, it was Mystik's maniacal actions that led Tonya to the hell hole she was in now, and if she surfaced again, there was no telling the trouble they could land in next. *Listen,* the alter, Mystik began speaking to Tonya's conscious, *you need to put an end to that girl's mouth. She's beginning to annoy me and if your bougie ass don't stop her, I will.*

"Why you sittin' over here looking all shady?" the loud-mouth woman had now walked over to Tonya, standing over her. Tonya didn't reply. She looked straight ahead without blinking, as if she were in a daze. "Oh, so you one of those deaf, dumb and ignorant chicks," the woman said matter-of-factly.

As soon as the words left her mouth, Tonya jumped up from her seated position, taking the other women in the cell by total surprise. They had no idea that this person was no longer Tonya; sure, it was Tonya's body, and even her voice they heard, however it was Mystik who had become fed up with the big mouthed woman. With the speed of lightening, she grabbed the butch-looking woman by her thick neck and began choking her, squeezing with the strength of a mad man— strength she never even knew she had. In an effort to defend herself, the woman began kicking her feet wildly, which caused Mystik to squeeze even harder.

Both women tumbled down to the floor with Mystik's hand still in a vice grip around the larger woman's throat. She had Tonya by at least 50 pounds, but her 50-pounds advantage was no good to her now that Mystik had taken control.

"Oh snap! That dark skin chick done went crazy y'all! She gonna kill Big Bertha!" one of the inmates shouted in panic.

"Somebody better stop her! She gonna kill her," another onlooker called out.

Tonya hadn't said a word since she'd been placed in the cell, nor had she bothered to befriend anyone. She needed her space, and at a time like this, she needed it even more so than usual. Unfortunately, Big Bertha had no clue what would happen if anyone dared to enter that space.

When she finally released Big Bertha's neck, she continued to hover over her in a stoic way. Then, surprising everyone, she spoke for the first time. "Don't you ever come at me on no simple shit like that again," she said, staring her directly in the eyes. "I realize you a simple bitch, but hopefully, your elementary ass can comprehend on this level. I don't do simple people and I especially don't do fake-ass, pretentious, grown-up adolescent-actin' kids like you. So, next time you see me sitting somewhere minding my own business, don't bring your ass in my face because that means the partition to my space has been invaded," Mystik spoke through clenched teeth.

"From now on, if I'm not talking to nobody, the partition is *closed*," she emphasized, before adding, "just in case your domestic ass didn't comprehend the first damn time!"

Shortly after hearing the commotion, a well-dressed gentleman appeared. He looked in and saw Tonya raising herself up off the floor, leaving a shocked, bruised Big Bertha lying there gasping for air. Mystik didn't respond to his presence, nor did she look in his direction. Instead, she sat back on the bunk they'd been sitting on before the rude interruption. And then, as if nothing had happened, she began bouncing her head to the imaginary music only they could hear. Music was their escape, and at times like this when they really needed separation from what was going on around them, they'd drown everything else completely out listening to the calming melodies that played in their private, mental, musical world.

The impeccable dressed man opened the cell door and locked his gaze on Tonya. "Come on and go with me," he ordered in a hesitant but stern tone. Mystik again spoke to Tonya. "I've handled her ass for you. You can take care of him, I'm exhausted. Tonya then looked over into the eyes of Captain Alexander Hunter, and his stern gaze revealed his authority.

It wasn't Officer Montauck, the officer she was expecting, but she knew the handsome man's request was nothing to feel threatened about. A woman like Tonya never obliged anyone's demand and she was quick to shut it down if anyone assumed otherwise. Even though the man standing before her wasn't who she'd been anticipating, his face was familiar and she'd seen the gentleman around the city occasionally.

He was never dressed in uniform, so she knew he was more of a superior figure than Officer Montauck. She didn't know him on a personal level, but nevertheless, she didn't feel any bad vibes either. So, without a second thought, she simply got up and followed him out of the cell.

***

Captain Alexander Hunter had encountered a lot of criminals. He'd been in law enforcement for a total of fifteen years and with his current precinct for eight. He'd worked his way up to Captain by taking down some of the biggest known criminals in the city. With one glance at the petite woman, he knew she was out of her element and surmised she'd been pushed to the edge by Big Bertha.

On the other hand, Big Bertha had become a regular visitor at the jail due to her constant fighting, and it didn't matter to her if they were male, female, big, or small. However, it appeared as though she'd finally met up with someone who wasn't intimidated by her size, and the Captain was clandestinely pleased to see someone had finally stood up to her while giving her a lesson about street life in the process.

He knew the young lady was no criminal but it was also plain to see she was no stranger to the likes of Big Bertha.

Captain Hunter led Tonya out of the cell and over to the interrogation room. He took a seat and motioned for her to sit in front of him.

"No, I'm good standing right here. You asked me to come with you, so here I am," Tonya said, slightly annoyed.

Her snotty demeanor didn't seem to bother Officer Hunter in the least bit; on the contrary, he found her candidness quite sexy. He raised his hands in the air in a surrendering gesture. "If you're more comfortable standing there, then by all means stay where you are. After seeing what you did to Big Bertha in the cell, I don't think anyone could force you to do anything anyway," he said, attempting to lighten her mood. "You wanna tell me what happened in there?"

Tonya looked at the Captain with unwavering eyes and said, "She got too comfortable in my space. If you need a formal statement, I have no problem with supplying you with one."

Captain Hunter stared at Tonya with lust dripping from his eyes and knew he had to get a grip on himself and do his job. It had been a very long time since a woman had caused him to have these kinds of feelings and he wasn't about to start again now.

"No need for a written statement. You can address the issue orally. I know Big Bertha's type and I don't see you as the type who likes drama," he said, while again finding himself starring at her a little longer than he should have.

Tonya was so into her own world, she never even noticed the longing look in his eyes. "Well, to put it simply, she got too close to my face for too long. I'm not a person who conforms to drama of any kind and I try to avoid it as best I can. But, if drama happens to find me, I escape away from it or quickly bring an end to it. My life has no room for drama, I have enough to deal with in reality," she said, while looking at Officer Hunter with an intense stare. She wanted to make sure he understood her completely. Tonya spoke very little, but when she did, she spoke with clarity.

This girl doesn't belong here, the Captain thought to himself; and the more he wondered, the more he felt the need to ask. So, he looked Tonya directly in the eyes. "Okay, so, you wanna tell me how a lady of your caliber ends up in a place like this?" His curiosity had gotten the best of him, yet his tone was filled with concern.

Giving him her undivided attention, Tonya took a seat in front of him; however, when she opened her mouth to speak, it was Mystik who had taken over the conversation. "I shot a bitch," she said in a nonchalant manner. The stoic look in her eyes revealed the hate embedded inside her soul.

Captain Hunter, although taken aback by Tonya's straight-forward admission, still thought she was the most beautiful, alluring woman he'd ever laid eyes on, nevertheless, the sudden change in her demeanor didn't match her outside appearance. It was weird but he could have sworn he'd heard her body calling out to him, however, he hadn't gotten where he was in life by being stupid and he wasn't about to start being stupid today.

Mystik knew the officer had no clue about the life "they" had lived and she didn't feel obligated to inform him. "Look, life is what it is, and for the moment, life has us here. I'm sure you can look at the records and read what our charges are," she said and crossed her legs, seductively. It didn't go unnoticed by the Captain, that she was speaking in third person term, but he was a little too distracted by her doe eyes to address anything else.

Wow, this woman makes the color orange look as though it was made to be worn exclusively by her, thought Captain Hunter.

Officer Hunter was tall, standing 6'3. Next to Tonya's petite 5'3 frame, he was a giant. He had a moderately, physically fit physique. His dark hair was cut low and close to his head, and his complexion added a natural, olive tan to his skin. With dark piercing eyes and a clean-shaven face, his appearance resembled that of a stellar actor. He was the epitome of handsome in every sense of the word.

Tonya looked as calm as a nun in Sunday school as she uncrossed her legs and sat straight up in her seat. Her gaze was still stuck on him but it wasn't as intense as it had been just seconds prior when Mystik appeared. Her beautiful, brown, doe eyes seemed to be shooting daggers into the depth of his soul, a look that hadn't been present before. But still, he couldn't shake the feeling that perhaps her being here was an awful mistake. *Maybe, she's trying to protect someone,* he thought. So, again, he interrogated her hoping to gain some true clarity.

"Look, Ms. Roberts, I recognize the type of lady you are and your type doesn't just end up in jail. I promise, I bring no grief your way, but I do bring a helping hand that I hope you'll accept," he stated sincerely.

This time when Tonya looked at him, she looked as if he'd suddenly grown two heads with horns. No matter how hard she tried, she could never stop "them" from invading her life. *No, Penni, keep your ass hidden. Mystik has done enough damage,* she ordered, hoping to keep her trio of personalities in check— unfortunately, to no avail.

Penni cocked her head slightly to the side and formed her lips into a slight smirk. "So...," she said sarcastically, "you're offering a helping hand, huh? What's gonna be waitin' behind the helpin' hand you offerin' so nicely? I don't do the snitchin' thing and even if I did I don't know nothin' about nobody in here."

Captain Hunter had been trained to analyze a person's personality and this chick had something major going on. He didn't know what that something was just yet, but he sure wanted the opportunity to investigate her further. "Well, look, you can hang out here for a while until the tempers cool down in the cell," he offered.

"While I appreciate your kindness, I'm fine to go back in. I really don't think I'll be having any more trouble," Tonya said with confidence, and just that quick, Penni was gone and Tonya was back.

Captain Hunter shook his head and replied. "No, Ms. Roberts, I don't think you have to worry about that," he paused… "it's the cellmates who have to worry," he said, followed with a smile. "Please, promise me you'll be good if I let you go back in there."

But, before Tonya could respond, Nisey, never one to be outdone, sprung up from her seat and gave a smile for the first time since they'd entered the room. "I'm always the good one. As long as they don't bring the drama to us, we'll be good."

Now, Captain Hunter was certain that the Ms. Roberts who had initially followed him to his office had "checked out" more than a few times since their conversation first began. *There's no way anybody can keep switching up like that...unless... Nah, can't be.* He pushed the thought to back of his mind, but he would, definitely, revisit it at a later time.

Just then, a female officer entered the room. "Hey Captain Hunter, what's going on?" she asked, not bothering to greet Tonya.

Tonya showed very little surprise hearing the officer refer to the man as *Captain,* because she had already figured him to be high in ranks. Her brain started running a mile a minute. Maybe he was sincere in his helping hand. If so, having a man of his ranking on her side could make getting out of here easier.

"Afternoon, Officer," the Captain replied. "I was just asking Ms. Roberts some questions. I heard a commotion while you were gone on your lunch break, so I went to investigate and found this little lady standing over a bruised Big Bertha," he informed her.

"Big Bertha is back in here again?" she asked, knowingly. Then, she turned her focus towards Tonya. "Roberts, you wanna tell me what that lil' altercation in the cell was all about?" Officer Grissom asked, looking Tonya up and down.

Tonya could tell that the female officer was trying to flaunt her authority, but she wasn't moved in the least bit. Staying true-to-self, she eyed the officer back with her usual nonchalant expression and said, "I already told the Captain what happened. He can relay the details to you.

Now, can I go back to the holding cell until my attorney comes?"

The officer wasn't completely caught off-guard by Tonya's sarcasm, and she could feel her disdain toward her. Besides, she'd encountered females like Tonya more times than she cared to remember, or so she thought. So without hesitation or stutter, she decided to let her know who was in charge. "Nah, Roberts, you won't be going back to the cell. We got a call from the hospital."

Karen D. Neal

SHEEBA/SHE'BAE

I can't believe Quanette tried to kill me… and after all I've done for her. I mean, I did spare her quite a few well-deserved ass whoopins'. Humph, they can continue to rally around waitin' on the demise of my life, but the joke will be on them, and I'll have the last laugh. She'bae don't die, she kills… And the first one on my list is Quanette's shady ass. And Davin got some nerve! Sittin' in here tryna to fool these people like he so concerned about me… He ain't foolin' me tho'…

As the recent events replayed themselves repeatedly in Sheeba's mind, her thoughts were suddenly interrupted. She began to feel pressure being applied over her eyes and the darkness became even darker. *What the hell? she thought… I know this fool didn't just put a pillow over my face…*

Sheeba hadn't opened her eyes yet, but she had been awake for the past 10 minutes. She had heard the nurse talking to Davin earlier and decided to see what his true reason was for staying at the hospital with her. Now, it was as clear as day— he was trying to finish her off.

Sheeba used all the strength she had and knocked Davin off of her, and in the process knocked the pulley over on the floor, along with Davin causing a loud crash.

Davin began hearing the voices inside his head that he hadn't heard in so long.

"See, this is the time to take over for your punk ass. You just allowed this crazy heifer to get the best of us and her ass is laying in the bed weak."

Darrius was the narcissistic personality to Davin and never viewed Sheeba as anyone, but She'bae. When Davin could not cope with his surroundings, it was Darrius who would come out and take control. Davin had been in control until the day he found himself at Tonya's house. Darrius had made several appearances since then.

Darrius jumped up off the floor just in time to see She'bae trying to snatch the IV from her arm. *I gotta get the jump on this fool*, he thought, as his adrenaline began to rush. But, before he could get back over to the bed, the nurse who had been in the room earlier burst in the door, taking he and She'bae both by surprise.

"OMG!" she exclaimed. "What's going on in here?" She looked from Sheeba to Davin and then back to Sheeba again. "Ma'am, you cannot take that out of your arm." Stephine was in shock at the sight of a very mobile, irate Sheeba, and she couldn't help but notice that a once depressed looking Davin now had the look of a wild animal after its prey.

"Get this shit outta my arm!" She'bae yelled. "This fool tried to suffocate me with a pillow," she said, pointing her index finger in Darrius' direction. She tried to get up, but two male orderlies restrained her.

Realizing he'd almost been caught, Darrius quickly allowed Davin to take control, as he began to play the "concerned-husband mode". He turned his attention to Stephine and remembered she was the same nurse who had shown him sympathy earlier that day. He shook his head, pitifully, and walked over to her.

"What kind of medicine is that running through her IV?" he questioned the nurse, somberly. Pouring it on thick, he pretended to wipe away a tear. "My wife seems to be having some mental side effects from the medication, or maybe it's a delayed reaction from the trauma she's gone through."

He paused as if he were in deep thought then rubbed his hands over his face showing his frustration. Releasing a heavy sigh, he continued. "When she woke up, she immediately started pulling on the IV, trying to pull it from her arm. I came over to stop her from pulling at the needle and that only made her aggressive behavior worse," he lied. "And, then-," he started to say.

But, before he could fabricate his story any further, She'bae interjected in a loud, angry tone, causing the nurse to jump from the sudden outburst.

"He's telling a bold-face lie! Davin, you were trying to kill me so you can be with that bitch, but She'bae will never die, boo! She'bae is a warrior!"

The nurse stared at Davin with a look of confusion plastered across her face. "Who is She'bae?" she asked curiously.

"That's her byname," he explained, "she uses it whenever she feels superior, and when she feels superior, she speaks in third person."

For a brief moment, it seemed as though the nurse had zoned out. Then as if a light bulb had suddenly came on, she said, "Wait a minute. Is she from Camden?"

Now, it was Davin's turn to look puzzled. "Yes, she is. And so am I. Do we know you?" he questioned, having no recollection of ever meeting the nurse before seeing her at the hospital.

Stephine began to shake her head no as she stepped away from Davin. "No, you don't know me at all. I have family members who have lived there for many years, and I used to visit my cousin, Quanette, during the summer months," she informed him. *

"Well, I doubt if either of you know me, but I do know of your reputations." Sheeba became even more irate to hear that Quanette and Stephine were cousins. "Somebody, anybody, please! Get this lady away from me!" she began hollering out. "She's gonna try and kill me just like my husband did! Please, get them out of my room! They're probably in cahoots." As she continued to cause a scene, people in the hallway began to whisper as they passed by her room.

Stephine couldn't believe what was happening— she had heard and seen enough! So, she looked to Dorinda. "I have to finish this charting. There's enough people in here to take care of the patient," she said, simultaneously preparing to exit the room. As Dorinda watched her friend/co-worker leave the room, she noticed that Stephine's attitude towards the situation had totally changed.

After Stephine had made it back to the nurses' station, she retrieved her cell phone from her purse, and scrolled through her directory in search of a phone number. After locating the number, she typed in a text message: 'Hi, this is Stephine. I know it's been a long time since we've talked, but please give me a call at this number asap, luv you, Cuz, even in distance'. Once she was done typing, she hit send.

***

Stephine and Quanette were two sisters' daughters. Stephine had grown up in Landsdowne, PA, and Quanette's family lived in the Haynes Projects in Camden, NJ, which was among the top five projects in crime rate in America. Even though they lived miles apart, the two cousins had been very close growing up. During summer breaks, they would take turns visiting one another, but as they grew older, the visits became few and far in between. As they grew older, reaching their early teens, the two had somewhat grown apart.

This particular summer while Stephine was visiting her cousin, they had been sitting out front on the stoop, chillin' with the rest of the kids in the neighborhood. The sun shone brightly as children played along the sidewalk, and the sounds of music could be heard from the cars that drove by slowly. All of a sudden, people started running towards what sounded like an altercation.

"Girl, what's goin' on over there now?" Quanette asked, as she stood up and began following the crowd.

Not wanting to be left alone on the stoop, Stephine followed her cousin.

When they approached the commotion that had gotten everyone's attention they saw a young girl lying on the ground. There was so much blood pouring out of her body, it was hard to tell where the wounds were. Stephine grabbed Quanette's hand and pulled her away from the scene, and they ran back in the direction of the stoop just as quickly as they'd left.

Upon entering the apartment, Quanette's heart felt as though it would beat right out of her chest. Stephine wasn't used to this type of violence and it showed from the fear in her eyes.

"Calm down, girl," Quanette told her, trying to conceal her own fear. "That was just She'bae actin' a fool 'cause some girl probably looked at Davin. She's so obsessed with that boy, she claims him as her private property and dares any girl to look at him. That girl must've looked at him," she explained to her cousin. "Don't worry tho'... You safe as long as you stay away from him," Quanette said, as if it was a normalcy; and, in the Haynes Projects, it was.

Stephine had never heard of such-a-thing happening in Landsdowne. So, that day, she vowed she would never visit her cousin again— at least not without the company of her parents.

***

Quanette was sweating like a pig running from a slaughter. She was almost done with her last route and she couldn't wait to get back to the post office to finish up for the day. She had been working at the post office for seven years, and although it was stressful, it provided a good life for her, her kids and her twin sister, Quanique. She never checked her phone while delivering mail because it was a distraction she didn't need. Besides, everyone who knew her knew not to call or text during the hours she worked her route.

She pulled up to the post office and grabbed all the empty trays from the delivered mail for that day. She hopped out of the vehicle and made her way inside where she placed the trays in a neat stack. She then took all the certified signatures and undelivered mail to the office for inventory.

Her phone, which had been in her jacket pocket, had vibrated twice since she'd arrived back to the post office, and now she could feel it vibrating for a third time. She was tired and sweaty and had no desire to hold a conversation with anyone; however, when she looked at the text and realized all of them had come from her cousin Stephine, she knew something had to be wrong.

Stephine: 'Hi, this is Stephine. I know it's been a long time since we talked, but please give me a call at this number asap. Luv you, Cuz, even in distance'.

"I hope she's okay," she whispered aloud.

She and her cousin had always been close but due to their work schedules, they hadn't spoken in a while. Her curiosity began to get the best of her and she was anxious to find out the details behind the urgent messages.

Quickly preparing for the next work day, she gathered all of the mail that had come in while she was out, and got it ready for the next day's deliveries. She glanced at the clock on the wall and smiled because her work day was over. *Finally*, she thought.

***

As Quanette dragged her tired body to her parked car, she reached in her pocket and retrieved her cell phone. After unlocking the car door and climbing inside, she dialed her cousin's number. She held the phone up to her ear hoping her cousin would answer rather than get her voicemail. But, to her surprise, there was already someone on the phone and the voice on the other end didn't belong to Stephine.

"Hello…," Quanette said in a questioning tone.

"Nette, where are you?"

Quanette took the phone away from her ear and looked at it as if she could see the person on the other end.

"Nique? How you get on the phone?" she asked. "I was trying to call Stephine."

"I called you, Nette… How else would I get you on the phone?" Nique asked in a frustrated tone.

Coincidentally, Nique had called Quanette at the same time Quanette was dialing Stephine. So, when Quanette thought she was placing a call, she had actually answered Nique's call unknowingly.

Quanique had been living with her sister for quite some time now and Quanette was very protective of her baby sister. Not only was she the eldest of the two, but Quanique wasn't 100% stable and she had a lot of mental issues. Growing up, there were many times Quanette covered for her sister and even got put on punishments for her. She didn't like seeing her little sister get into trouble and covering for her had always been easy to do, especially since they were identical twins. The sisters had been born 3 hours apart but Quanette was born first, and according to close friends and family members she'd been her sister's keeper since birth…

Karen D. Neal

"Push... Push... Push..."

"What the hell you think I'm doin'? Arggggg..."

Pregnant with twins, Rochelle had been in labor for twenty-one hours. She had already given birth to one of the babies 3 hours ago, but had suddenly gone into a critical state. To the doctor's dismay, the second baby still had the umbilical cord wrapped around her neck, along with part of the first baby's cord.

The births had been difficult for mother and babies, and this last hour depended upon life or death for the young mother and her unborn baby. She had defiantly refused to have a C-section. She had said she was not distorting her body any further with these babies. She'd been quite bitter about having twins and never tried to hide the fact that she was not happy about being tied down with two children.

"Ms. Johnson, we can see her head. Please, push with everything you have," the doctor coached her.

Rochelle gave one final, huge push and she could feel her vagina as it stretched and ripped apart. She screamed out profanities as the excruciating pain surged through her lower body. And just when she felt as though she'd pass out, the baby slid out of her slowly. Although the newborn was alive, her tiny frame was still and her skin was blue in color.

The medical team quickly went to work trying to save the baby's life. They removed the cords from around the baby's neck and then rushed her to ICU. Once they cleaned her up, they placed her in an incubator beside her sister and watched as the older sister began to cry right away. They put them into the same incubator and witnessed the older sister grab her little sister's hand and both babies peacefully drifted off to sleep.

That had been 28 years ago, but to this very day, Quanette was still her sister's keeper.

Because of the complications during labor, Quanique had suffered with brain damage which led to her being mentally challenged. The twin sisters had grown up in the Haynes projects in Camden, NJ, with their mother, Rochelle, and through childhood the girls had been inseparable. However, it was Quanique who kept them both in trouble.

When they graduated high school, Quanette got a job with the USPO and moved them both out into their own place. She never looked back, although they were only minutes away.

Quanique, however, would make frequent trips back to their roots. Unbeknownst to her sister, she would hang out there during the day while Quanette worked.

One day shortly after they'd moved away, Quanique began visiting their old neighborhood when she befriended She'bae who had always mistaken her to be Quanette. Loving all of the attention she received as her sister, Nique never corrected her because for once she felt as though she was part of the in-crowd.

Quanette rolled her eyes, while shaking her head. "Nique, I'm just leaving work and need to call you back. Stephine keeps calling me and I need to see what's up with her since she hardly ever calls."

"Oh, so you just gonna put somebody else's need before mine? Your own sister?" Nique pouted.

"Girl, don't start with that nonsense," Quanette replied in an irritated tone. "It ain't even like that and you know it," she snapped. "Anyway, I'll see you when I get to the house," she told her and ended the call before Nique could respond.

***

On edge because of the dramatic events that had taken place, Stephine continued to chart the patients' info into the data system. Her mind couldn't help but replay She'bae's accusation against her husband.

After everything had calmed down in Sheeba's room, Dorinda made her way down the hallway and over to her friend's desk.

"Stephine, girrrl," she said in a dramatic voice, "do you know those crazy people in that room? That girl is certifiable crazy! I don't blame her husband for tryna kill her!" she added becoming more animated. "I'd be trying to get rid of her crazy ass too!" Stephine pushed her seat back from her desk and grabbed the mug of coffee she'd been drinking from all morning. She held her finger up at Dorinda indicating she needed to take a drink of her coffee before continuing.

Dorinda knew her colleague all too well and knew whenever she paused to sip her coffee, some juicy details were sure to follow. She got herself a Coke and took a seat next to Stephine eager to hear the details.

"I don't know them personally, and I haven't seen either of them in over fifteen years, but they used to live in the same neighborhood as my cousin out in the Haynes projects," Stephine informed her.

Dorinda became quite and her facial expression appeared perplexed. In deep contemplation, she tried to figure out where she'd first heard of the Haynes projects before. Suddenly, as if a light bulb had come on, the puzzled look on her face turned to a look of recognition as she recalled exactly where the neighborhood was located. "Girrrl, I know where you talkin' 'bout. Shut the front door!" she said in a raised tone, now remembering when she'd first heard of the notorious Haynes projects. "Those are some crazy people in that area, but that couple don't look like they are from there. But, on the other hand, that crazy chick was actin' like the girl I've heard about from that same area. I lived close to that area, but my mom always forbade me to go near there," she told Stephine. "There was this crazy girl who lived in that projects with a reputation for cuttin' folks, and I wasn't tryna have no cuts on me, child." Dorinda stated, while batting her eyes dramatically.

Stephine pushed her seat back from the desk and jumped up from her chair. "Oh, my God! That's that same crazy girl in the room. They called her She'bae, but she's signed in as Sheeba Walker, so I didn't recognize her until I went in and heard her talking in third person referring to herself as She'bae!" Stephine was baffled and she couldn't believe that the patient and the crazy girl they'd heard about was one-in-the-same. "You noticed how I turned around and walked out right?" she looked to Dorinda and asked.

Dorinda shook her head yes and continued with her story. "My mom told me how she beat a girl down one day at the bus stop. The girl had just moved into the neighborhood and didn't know how crazy She'bae was about other girls talking to her boyfriend. I don't know if she survived or not, but my mom told me She'bae cut the poor girl pretty badly, and shortly afterwards, her family moved away."

Stephine pursed her mouth as she tilted her head and said, "I was there. I was visiting my cousin that day and I saw everything."

Dorinda, being the drama queen she is, covered her mouth and gasped. "OMG...girl! You knew she was a lunatic, so why didn't you warn a sista'?" she said dramatically. Shaking her head from side to side, she found it hard to believe a woman would be so obsessed over a man that she'd risk her freedom. "I was talking to her husband, trying to get him to leave so she would calm down, but he's determined not to leave her side. She definitely has a man who loves her."

Stephine looked at Dorinda like she had really lost her mind. "Girl, please… if anything he wants to watch that crazy fool die so he can finally live. According to the stories I've heard in the past, if she's still as possessive as she was back then, I know his life has been pure hell."

The two women continued to chat until Stephine received the call she had been waiting on. She looked down to assure it was her cousin and excused herself to the back, in case the doctors happen to come in. Stephine didn't give Quanette a chance to speak before she began throwing out questions one after the other.

"Nette, you remember that crazy girl who lived in the same neighborhood as you in the Haynes Projects? The one who would kill anybody who looked at her boyfriend too long?" There was a pause on the line which caused Stephine to become even more dramatic. "Quanette. Hello. Hell-ooo..."

Quanette removed the phone from her ear due to the volume in Stephine's voice, but she could also tell her cousin was clearly upset and this really concerned her. "Stephine, calm down and start over. I just got off and I'm too tired to play guessing games right now. Now to answer the first question you asked me, I first need to know exactly what crazy girl you're referring to... There were a lot of crazy girls in the Haynes Projects so you need to be a little more specific," she said in a soft tone, hoping Stephine would calm down as well.

Stephine huffed in agitation. She took a deep breath and began from the beginning.

"Okay... Do you remember that summer I visited you and we were sitting on the steps when this girl cut another girl at the bus stop because she was talking to her boyfriend? Y'all called her Bae Bae or something like that..."

There was a slight hesitation on the line before Quanette finally spoke up. "Oh, you're talking about She'bae's crazy ass. What about her?"

Stephine sighed with ease as she began to inform Quanette about She'bae. "She was admitted to the hospital down here yesterday and she'd been shot. I didn't recognize her when she was first admitted, and honestly, it didn't look like she was going to survive. But, that ain't even the half! A little while go she went ham and started wilding out on her husband!" Stephine said. "And, might I add, she's still in the ICU!

There was a gasp on the other end of the phone as Quanette's voice boomed through the receiver. "What husband?"

Stephine looked at the phone like it was hot as she snatched it away from her ear. "Her husband who's here with her now. The one whose ass she beat while she's in critical condition!" she reiterated. "She's just as crazy now as she was then!" Stephine added, in an unbelievable tone.

"What time do you get off?" Quanette asked. "Quanique is at the house with my kids and I need to get there and make sure everything is okay. Give me a call when you get off and we can meet at the deli around the corner from the hospital."

Stephine wanted to know more about the strange couple, so she agreed to meet with her cousin at seven-thirty.

TONYA

Tonya was relieved to be in her own home, and her body welcomed the hot water that cascaded around her body as she soaked in the tub of lightly scented bubble bath, washing away the remnants of the past three days. A representative at the hospital had called her lawyer after Sheeba regained consciousness, he'd gotten her charges reduced to self-defense. Never once had she felt the need to tell her lawyer she was innocent. She'd realized the girl who shot She'bae had saved her life, so in return, she would never tell anyone she wasn't the person holding the weapon.

Since it had been Tonya's resident, they had arrested her for the time being. Nonetheless, Davin knew she wasn't the shooter, but she knew he didn't want any more heat than necessary aimed in his direction. At the time, she didn't know he had confessed to pulling the trigger himself, causing a major confusion in the investigation as to who the shooter really was.

Now, finally back in the comforts of her peaceful abode, she toweled herself dry followed by some moisturizer for her skin. As she sat, lost in her own thoughts, her mind began to wander back in time…

Tonya looked up and saw a girl approaching who appeared to be the same age as she was; or, at least, very close to it. She couldn't help but be consumed by fear as this colorful creature came towards her. She'bae was dressed in a bright orange skirt, and a blue jean vest which opened to a tight fuchsia colored bra— She'bae was exposing more meat than a meat packaging company. Her hair was two shades of fuchsia, in a bob-type style, with purple ends, and she looked two kinds of crazy.

The doorbell rang interrupting her thoughts and she got up to grab her housecoat while wondering whom it could be. She peeked through the peek-hole before beginning to unlock the door.

"So, your crazy wife survived her near death like I survived mine when she tried to end my life. At least she won't have to go through reconstructive surgeries and months of rehabilitation to be human again." Tonya said with conviction.

Davin stepped inside the door and closed it, never taking his eyes off Tonya. "It's you. I can't believe after all these years, you're standing right in front of me. I wanted to see you so badly, but between your Dad and She'bae, I didn't stand a snowball's chance in hell. Where did you go after you were released from the hospital?" he asked, never pausing his words for an answer. "Even though your Dad threatened to kill me if I ever came around you again, I continued to search for you, but it was like you guys had dropped off everyone's radar. They never came back after the incident with She'bae and I never heard anything from you or your family again until I saw you in the grocery store. Even then I never realized who you were until you revealed your identity later here at your place."

Davin wanted so badly to hold Tonya now that he knew who she was, but fearing it would set her off and cause one of her multiple personalities to appear, he quickly dismissed the thought. Tonya looked somewhat mystified but despite her feelings, she still asked Davin to have a seat and offered him a drink. Remembering the events of the previous day, he thought it best to decline her offer; besides, he needed a clear head to deal with the crazy situation that had somehow found its way into his life.

Tonya made herself a drink and took a seat on the couch beside the chair Davin had chosen to sit in.

"Okay, Davin or Darrius, or whoever the hell else you may be," Tonya said with no consideration or regards to the fact that she too was prone to the mental illness. "So you think you're owed an explanation about me and my family, huh? Well, let's see," she said, as she sat with her legs crossed and took a sip of her drink. Then, as if she'd suddenly had an instant mood swing, she went over to her stereo and turned the music on. Rhianna and Kanye's hit single *FourFiveSeconds* softly played as she refreshed her drink. She returned to her seat and got comfortable, removing her shoes and placing her feet up on the coffee table. She lay back holding her drink.

Davin couldn't help but notice how soft her feet looked, and her toenails were immaculately manicured. They looked so tasteful, he had to really restrain himself as he watched her sip from the drink in her hand.

"Okay, let's be clear..." Tonya said in a defensive tone, "what happened to me was more than just *an incident*," she told him, mimicking what she thought to be a lack of seriousness toward the situation. "First of all, I didn't fall on the ground and merely scrape my face— your crazy ass friend sliced me up hoping I would die," Tonya began in a frustrated yet calm tone of voice. "I would classify that as an, oh... let me see" she said, sitting back in a relaxing state as if she were in deep thought. "Personally, I would call it a traumatic day; the day my life changed forever, but nevertheless, a day I had to endure to become the woman I am today.

And, as for what happened that day? I can't tell anyone what transpired after the attack on me. Everything that took place up to that point left my mind. My mom told me I was driven to the hospital by car, because the ambulance would have taken too long or not come at all. I don't have any recollection of that day, only what was told to me. And from what I hear, it wasn't a pretty picture. But then again, I'm sure you already know that.

I do however, have memories of the nightmares I've had nightly, of waking up looking into the mirror to see a scarred face. I remember the many nights of waking up with anxiety, not being able to breath, with no escape from the unforeseen fear. Although the surgery was able to repair the scars that were on my face, nothing will ever be able to repair the scars of my pain. I spent months in facility after facility, having reparation on top of reparation. I've gone through years of having my mom breathing down my back constantly, because she refused to let me out of her sight. I finally moved out and took control of the life that's been given to me. I realized nothing would ever take away the pain I have endured."

Davin wanted so badly to erase all the nightmares she'd had; he wanted to go back in time to a place where she was young and carefree; to tell her he was there for her and he would never let anything bad happen to her again. He wished he could kiss away the hidden pain masked behind her big, dark, brown eyes. He wanted her to let him inside the gate to the little girl who needed to be reassured the danger was no longer there. But, at the moment, he knew touching her wasn't an option. The gate-keeper or 'host' would never allow him entrance into their world right now. He knew because of his personal experience with the forced illness of Dissociative Identity Disorder. Yes, he too had the mental disorder, so he knew first-hand the fight within this beautiful lady who sat next to him.

Unbeknownst to Tonya, Davin had begun counseling just before he'd decided to leave Sheeba/She'bae'. He'd realized it wasn't normal to be in such a controlling relationship, so when he'd started having memory lapses of small occurrences in his daily life, he sought help. It was then he'd become aware of his illness and he was determined to take control of his own life. He'd attended seminars as well as doing extensive research on the condition. He'd had control over them until that day Tonya came back into his life. Her personalities had forced his own personalities out of integration, but yet and still, he knew to approach the host accordingly.

"Tonya, are you in therapy for yours?"

Tonya stared Davin in the eyes with a knowing look and precisely asked, "Am I in therapy for what?"

Davin returned the knowing look and replied. "Are you receiving therapy for your Dissociative Identity Disorder?"

Tonya became more relaxed at his response. She had suspected that he also suffered with some type of disorder, but she had learned to never assume anything until given facts. She'd also learned through counseling to help others with the problem by sharing her own experience.

"I began therapy a year ago, but I had long recognized a problem existed. I had so much anger inside of me, but I could hide the anger behind my work and hide the pain behind my smile. I realized I could allow what happened to me to take over, or I could go to battle and gain control of my life.

I began releasing pent-up hurt by hurting others. I blamed men for my pain, beginning with my father. I blamed him for losing his job and moving us to such an unsafe neighborhood. I blamed you for the actions of your then girlfriend who almost ended my life. There were more men in between who I blamed, though not many. Each gained my trust in some way, but like always, I ended up realizing that Tonya, and only Tonya, is here for Tonya. I guess my therapy sessions were all in vain once I saw you again," she concluded.

Tonya got up to refill her glass. She felt so at ease, but she also felt the need to finally release the emotions that she'd kept buried inside her for so many years. She walked back over to the couch with her drink in hand, a cold look in her eyes. Davin recognized the look because he had once worn that same look and knew all too well the emotions behind the empty look.

"Tonya, are you currently in counseling for your illness?" Tonya looked at Davin emotionless and casually asked. "Is that what you call it? Well, Davin… Oh, but wait, I am talking to 'the host' Davin, right?" Tonya asked with a facetious tone laced with sarcasm. "I keep myself under control most of the time. I admit to a little slippage here and there, but only if pushed."

With his head tilted to one side, Davin looked at Tonya with a questioning expression on his face. "How did I push you and all I did was ask you out to lunch?" The simple question threw the entire conversation in a totally different direction.

"I suppose the same way you talking to me at the bus stop pushed your nutty girlfriend to nearly kill me," she replied in a nonchalant manner. "You're such an expert on this "illness" as you like to refer to it, yet you don't even realize what can push a person backwards?" Tonya placed her drink down on the coffee table and placed her right finger under her chin as if in deep thought. "Could it be, when a person is faced with the component of a traumatic experience, the memories come flooding back?" she asked. "Oh wait, hot damn I got it!" she blurted out, never giving him a chance to reply.

"When you realize you have no one, you can become hollow, and you become hollow because all of your emotions have been stolen. I, for one, don't welcome back stolen goods. Once those emotions have been stolen they can never be stolen from me again. I have no clue how many emotions a human comes equipped with, but you better believe all of mine are gone," she said with conviction.

"Now... enough talk about me, what was the chic's name who came in and saved my life? I don't welcome new people into my life, but I do have enough common courtesy to thank them if they save it."

As Davin spoke, he seemed to become distant. "Thanks for not ratting her out. Her name is Quanette," he told her, "she used to live in the Haynes Projects when we were younger, and she always wanted to be accepted by She'bae and her friends. I always knew she was off, but I never knew to what extent. She just...never, never seemed quite all together, if you know what I mean."

Tonya looked a little puzzled. "Well, even though I never knew her name, I knew her face.

She's our postal lady, and I don't think she would've ever landed a job delivering mail if she wasn't all there," she said followed by a light chuckle.

Now it was Davin's turn to look puzzled. "You must be mistaken. Quanette still hangs out in the Haynes Projects. Some of my boys have even mentioned how she's there from sun up till sun down most days."

Tonya hunched her shoulders up in a matter-of- fact manner. "Oh well, I guess she has a twin who looks just like her, because I know my postal lady when I see her. She's been on this route ever since I moved here three years ago."

Davin's phone began to ring, and when he looked at the screen, he saw it was an incoming call from the hospital. "Excuse me, I need to take this call."

"Hello, Davin speaking." There was a pause on the other end and Davin's heart skipped a beat as he waited to hear what the hospital could be calling him for. Had he been able to see through the phone, he would have seen Nurse Dorinda fanning herself from hearing his voice.

"Mr. Williams, I'm calling to let you know your wife has been sedated and we've finally gotten her to calmed down. The doctors would like to meet with you here in her room tomorrow morning, concerning some other issues that pertain to your wife." Davin let out a breath that was hard to distinguish if it was a breath of relief or defeat.

"Sure, I can meet with them. What time will they be making rounds?"

"Rounds will begin at 7 a.m., sir, but I can't exactly say what time they'll get to her room. But, what I can tell you is that all rounds have usually been made by 11 o'clock," she informed him.

"Great, I'll be there by 6:45 in the morning. Thanks for calling, um… excuse me, I'm sorry, but I didn't get your name," he said in a polite tone.

The voice on the other end giggled. "How rude of me not to introduce myself before addressing the issue. I'm Dorinda."

"Okay, Dorinda. If there's nothing else, please confirm my arrival time in the morning with the doctors."

"I'll be sure to let the doctors know, Mr. Williams," the nurse said.

"Oh, and, Dorinda," he called out before ending the call, "thanks for calling."

"My pleasure, Sir," Dorinda said and disconnected the lines.

Davin was about to go back inside until Tonya met him at the door with her purse in one hand while holding his car keys in the other.

"Sorry to rush you off, but I have some errands to run. Please, keep that crazy wife of yours away from me," she scolded with a frown.

And just like that, Tonya disappeared onto the elevator. She didn't bother to give Davin a chance to get on before pushing the button which caused the doors to close right in his face. As the elevator descended to the ground floor, she said a silent prayer, hoping he'd get the unsubtle hint and leave her alone once and for all. After spending all those hours in a holding cell packed with people, what she craved more than anything was solitude.

DAVIN

Davin was disheartened at the awful appearance of the neighborhood he'd grown up in. Slowly, he cruised the streets while reliving the days he'd lived there. In his opinion it was a living hell, and judging from the state it was in now, it seemed to be worse than before. *How can the government allow such an area to even exist?* He thought to himself. But then he remembered where the location was. This was a section of the city that had been forgotten by many, avoided by others, and occupied by the desperate.

As he continued driving slowly, he saw one of his homeboys, Trek, riding on a homemade bike. He stopped his car and hopped out to give Trek some love. Despite how his old friends had decided to live, he had never turned his back on them, and he always treated them as if he'd never moved away.

Trek had on a pair of dirty, torn jeans and an old baseball cap that use to be white but was now brown, sat atop his head. He reeked of alcohol and held onto a brown paper bag that obviously held a forty-ounce can of beer.

"Davin! What's good, my dude?" he greeted in a cheerful voice. The smile on his face was evidence he was happy to see his old friend. "I ain't seen much of you since you moved uptown on us little folks."

I'm the same every time you see me!" Davin said in his own defense. "The question is, when are you going to get off of that bike, clean yourself up, and use the smarts you've always had?"

Davin stuck his fist out to Trek for a pound, despite the odor emancipating through his childhood friend's pores. Trek was the same age as Davin, but looked to be fifteen years older. They had grown up close and everyone had hopes of Trek earning a spot on the PGA Tour. When the children in his neighborhood found out he was playing golf, they all begin to tease him, calling him a wimp.

Trek loved sports in general and always put his best into any sport he played. Playing golf was unheard of in their neighborhood, but Trek's mom had entered him into a First Tee Program one summer to have him closer to her during her workdays. The director saw a gift in Trek and having a love for golf himself, he became a mentor for the eight- year-old boy.

Trek had been an all-around star back in school and he'd earned a scholarship to Rutgers University in Camden to play on the Scarlet Knights golf team. He had the brain for getting into the school and the skills for playing the game of golf. He could easily drive a ball over 350 yards, which was a rare gift, in and of itself— and even more rare in a teenage kid from the projects. Yet, Treks talent had gained the attention of colleges while he broke driving records, putting records and made golf his top sport in high school.

He'd broken the cardinal rule and began dating a girl from the Bell Meadows country club where he had been working as a caddy after starting school at Rutgers University in New Brunswick, New Jersey. Although his skills were great and he'd been welcomed into the school, his color was never welcomed at the country club. He was found behind that same country club bound by both hands. His feet had been hanging from a tree branch and he was naked as the day he was born, and there were welts all over his body. He was never the same again, physically or mentally.

"So, Trek, does that girl, Quanette, who used to always wanna be around She'bae still come around here?"

Trek looked a little confused at first. "You mean that lil' short yellow honey who comes around? Acts a little slow?"

"Yeah, yeah, that's the one," Davin agreed.

"She still comes around but her name ain't Quanette, that's her sister's name, man," Trek corrected him. "Her name is Quanique."

Now, Davin really looked confused and his mind wandered back to when he lived in the neighborhood. "I don't think the girl I'm talkin' about has a sister."

Trek gave Davin a dead-pan look. "Well, how many girls do you know who have names like Quanette and Quanique?" he asked with a hint of sarcasm. But to answer your question, they are sisters. They're identical twins to be exact. You'll know them apart though, trust me on that one, my man. Quanique is slow, and Quanette is anything but slow. No one ever sees Quanette on this side of town since they moved away as teenagers," Trek informed him, catching Davin by total surprise. He looked at Davin curiously and asked, "Why, what did she do?"

Davin couldn't believe what he was hearing, but he knew Trek had no reason to mislead him.

"Why would you ask what she did?" he asked inquisitively.

Trek gave a slow, crooked grin. "Man, that chick act all quiet, but she crazy for real, man! She always seein' shit other people around never sees. She been doing that shit so long, don't nobody even pay attention to her no more.

Hearing this revelation relieved Davin to some degree, but he still needed to know more about her. He asked Trek to have a beer with him and of course he agreed.

They went to a little sports bar around the corner since it wasn't too busy during this time of the day. In fact, it was pretty empty tonight with only the bartender and a few patrons. A couple of guys were playing pool, with just a few people scattered about. Davin and Trek chose a table in the back, but the door was still in view.

Davin and Trek ordered their beers along with some hot wings. As they sat talking about the old days, Quanique's name came back up. Davin had to find out the connection between this chic, Quanique, and Sheeba getting shot.

"So, Trek, why don't I remember these twins if they from the Haynes Project?"

Trek gave Davin a knowing look. "Because She'bae's crazy ass made sure no other girls were around you fool. Have you forgotten how she would mess a girl up just for looking in your direction? What it was is that most people didn't realize it was two of them because they were identical, and the slow one, Quanique, is the one that hung around with She'bae and her crew. She was always quiet and kept a cap pulled over her eyes. She never talked and she was usually just there, wanting to be a part of the clique."

As he pondered momentarily, the sudden recognition hit Davin like a ton of bricks.

"Oh, you mean the little short cute girl who went to the store for them all the time, the one who was basically their flunky."

Trek snapped his finger and said, "By George, I think you've got it!"

Davin took a wing from the plate. "OK, you funny man. I get your point."

They heard the door open and looked up simultaneously, just in time to see Quanette and another young lady walking in. Davin nearly choked on his wing while Trek looked back to see what had Davin's attention.

"Oh, that's Quanette right there, that's not Quanique," Trek said, noticing the confused look on Davin's face.

"How can you tell them apart if they're identical?" Davin quizzed.

Trek took a swig of his beer and sat back sucking on a wing bone as if he'd never get anything else to eat. "Quanette is the stuck-up bitch who thinks her shit smell like roses. Quanique ain't quite right, but she's more down to earth and ain't forgot where she came from."

The wheels in Davin's brain began to turn as he tried to think of a reason to go over and say something to the girls, and get Quanette's attention in the process. His main goal was to gauge her reaction to seeing him.

Finally, he stood up from the table and went over with the pretense of knowing her, but when he got to the table, he realized the other girl was one of the nurses from the hospital. He almost didn't recognize her out of her uniform. Now, he was able to formulate an alibi for approaching their table.

"Excuse me, Miss. Are you one of the nurses taking care of my wife at Cooper Memorial hospital?"

Stephine had seen Davin approaching them and became nervous. "Yes, I am, Mr. Williams."

Davin held his hand up to stop her. "Please, call me Davin. I just wanted to thank you for all your care." He never took his eyes off of Quanette, and she stared right back at him, allowing him to finish addressing her cousin.

"Hi, Davin, you probably don't remember me but we grew up together in the Haynes Project. I'm so sorry to hear about your wife being ill."

Davin looked Quanette square in the eyes and realized she wasn't the one who had pulled the trigger. He decided to probe a little bit more in an inconspicuous manner.

"Forgive me for being so rude, but I keep looking at you because you look so familiar to me."

Quanette gave a nervous smile in Davin's direction. "We both use to live in the Haynes projects as kids," she responded.

Davin faked a smile of recognition and snapped his fingers. "I remember you. Didn't you have a sister? A twin sister who hung around Sheeba?"

It was now Quanette's turn to look perplexed. "I'm sorry, I don't know anyone by the name of Sheeba."

Trek couldn't stand it any longer and needed another beer. After retrieving his beer, he went over to help shed some light for Quanette. "Hey, ladies. Quanette, I know this may come as a surprise to you, but Sheeba is none other than She'bae. Everyone remembers the notorious She'bae with all the hell she raised about this man right here," Trek said, grabbing Davin and then patting him on the shoulder in a friendly manner.

Quanette's face feigned with surprise. "Oh my goodness. You're Davin Williams, the guy She'bae claimed for herself! I never knew her government name, but what ever happened to her?"

Davin looked at Stephine and answered, "I married her which brings me back to this young lady with you," he said, turning his attention towards Stephine.

"Oh, this is my first cousin, Stephine," Quanette said, introducing Stephine to both Davin and Trek. "You guys don't remember her from the summers she used to visit me? We always stayed close to home or right on the stoop."

Trek looked over at Stephine and licked his lips, lustfully. "I would have remembered this beautiful lady if I ever saw her."

Quanette began to loosen up and she became more relaxed. She looked at Trek and let out a friendly laugh. "Trek, what's been up with you? I'm so sorry to hear about the demise of your golf career. I remember the skills you had on that course and it's a shame the world didn't get to see it," she said sympathetically.

Trek, on the other hand, hated to be reminded of what he *used* to be. He felt like a shell of the young man he had been just a few years ago. He was a twenty-eight-old man who felt completely useless and washed up. Not knowing how to deal with the feeling of failing, he hid his disappointment behind drinking, morning, noon and night. He couldn't recall a second when he didn't have alcohol in his system.

"How you been doin', Quanette? You sho' lookin' scrumptious girl," Trek flirted. "The post office must be treatin' you good. I see Quanique on a daily basis, but I haven't seen you since you guys moved out."

Quanette tilted her head with a confounded expression on her face.

"How do you see Nique everyday Trek?" Quanette asked with continued bemusement."

"She hangs out on the stoop with the old gang who still lives there," Trek said, impetuously.

She looked at Trek with a disgusted frown and turned her nose up. "Are you saying my sister is over there with *you people* every day? How is that possible when she's home babysitting for me?"

Trek gave her a stern, candid look then said, "When a crack ho wants that hit, she'll make a way, so I guess your kids have been pretty much babysitting their damn selves." Quanette had struck a nerve in Trek when she spoke of him as a lowlife and he didn't care to hide his irritation. "Davin, man, I'll see you back at the table, 'cause I ain't tryna talk to this stuck-up bitch."

With that said, he went back over to the table and turned up the empty beer bottle. He slammed the bottle back down on the table and yelled out for service. "Can I get another beer over here, please!"

Davin looked over to Quanette and apologized for Trek's behavior.

"You don't need to apologize to me for him. An attitude is expected from a lowlife like him."

Now, Davin could see the difference between Quanette and Quanique. The young lady who pulled the trigger didn't have the same hateful look in her eyes as the young lady standing before him. Trek had been right all along and the sisters were indeed identical twins, except this one had personal issues with her old neighborhood. The few seconds he'd looked into her eyes, exhibited the look of a terrified little girl. He recognized the look of a person trying to escape their past in Quanette's eyes. He also understood, but he didn't appreciate how she'd done his boy. He thanked Stephine once again and told Quanette it was good seeing her again before turning to walk back to his table.

Davin saw the look of defeat on his friend's face as he approached their table, but as he got closer, he also noticed a faint glimpse of the look of pride that been buried deep inside, behind ounces of beer. He took a seat just as the waiter was bringing another beer to the table. "We won't be needing those, just bring the bill," he told the waiter.

Trek looked at Davin with a frown on his face. "Damn, Davin, you don't invite a man out for beer and just buy him one. Where they do that at? 'Cause I don't need to be nowhere near there," Trek said jokingly.

"We'll have plenty of beer where we're going, let's just get out of here." Davin said. After reaching in his pocket, he threw two twenties on the table and walked out with a pissed off Trek on his trail.

TONYA

Tonya had circled the block allowing Davin time to leave. She didn't trust her alters around him. She hated to admit to herself that she was going to have to restart therapy, but with the mess her alters had her in, at this point, she knew it was inevitable.

She was relieved She'bae had survived, and the level-headed Tonya prayed she would make a complete recovery. She had been playing a dangerous game with so many guys, but none of them ever tried to press charges on her after the crazy, nightly escapades spent in her special room. She would simply email them the next morning, sending them the pictures she'd snapped of them in various, compromising poses, while handcuffed to her bed.

Although most people viewed her to be a career woman, no one knew her real money came from the many guys she was blackmailing. She would collect as much as $50,000 from each victim, which was deposited directly into her account monthly.

Aside from that, she was able to live off the income she made as a Legal Assistant for a team of attorneys in Camden. She was great at what she did, but she knew her position there was only temporary.

After reaching her goal of $1,000,000.00 she planned to start her own business far away from the madness. She was over halfway there with $700,000 in her account. Actually, she could be content with that amount if she could just get out of this mess. She would give her notice as soon as everything cleared up with this Davin/Sheeba situation and move far away and make a brand-new start and a happy life for herself; she had actually considered going back to school to become an attorney herself.

Tonya's phone began playing FourFiveSeconds causing her to roll her eyes in an irritated manner. She knew Mystik had changed the ringtone to her preference song during her presence, but she didn't have time to worry about that at the moment though. The display showed the police department calling and she knew it was officer Montauk.

***

"Hello," Tonya greeted the caller. The voice on the other end was so deep and smooth and she could feel Penni trying to surface as he called her name.

"Hello, may I speak with Ms. Tonya Johnson?"

"Yes, this is she, and who are you?" Damn, Mystik was back and just that quick, she was taking the lead. The tone in her voice made the officer cautious about his next question.

"I'm calling in hopes you'll agree to meet me outside of the precincts. I promise, I'm on your side, and I give you my word that I'll do all I can to help keep you free."

When Mystik realized the voice on the other line didn't belong to Officer Montauk, she allowed her alter to fade. It was Captain Hunter, so she allowed Tonya to handle it from here.

"Um, sure, but we have to meet in a very public place," Tonya spoke as soon as she knew Mystik was gone.

Officer Hunter gave a light chuckle and replied, "That won't be a problem, tell me where you'd like to meet, and please, call me Gerald."

The Captain was being very polite and he seemed easy enough to deal with, however, Tonya wasn't about to let her guards down that easily. "There's a little deli on 5th and Main, I'll meet you there in 30 minutes, Captain Hunter." She hung up before he could reply, because the way she saw it, if he was serious about helping her he wouldn't have a problem with meeting right away.

DAVIN

Davin and Trek were sitting in Davin's living room drinking a few beers. Davin had invited a couple of guys over and he'd given Trek some gym shorts, a jersey, and some Jordan's to change into.

Trek was beyond surprised when Davin took him to his home and threw the clothes and shoes at him while telling him happy birthday. "It's not my birthday, dude, but I 'preciate the hook-up."

Davin gave a smile and said, "Yeah, it's your new birthday. Just go in the bathroom and take a shower, man, we've got company coming over in a few minutes."

"Aww, hell! Trek said excitedly. "My dawg done got us some ladies coming over here! You don't have to tell me twice," he said as he turned to walk away. Just before he reached the bathroom, he turned back around to face Davin. "Hey, you got some of that good smelling shit I can put on afterwards?" he asked, feeling like his old self again.

"Just go get your ass washed and the funk will go away! Trust me, man." Davin laughed as he got a card table ready and put 50 Cent on the iPod.

***

The two guys Davin had invited over were actually professional instructors whom he'd befriended from Galloping Hill Golf Course, and personal friends of his. Trek was highly disappointed because what he thought were going to be two flyy chics, turned out to be two dudes Davin golfed with. He was enjoying the conversation as they sat drinking, playing cards, and discussing the sport he knew inside out. He was really feeling like a part of him had come back to life. For the moment, he no longer felt like the lowlife who rode the bike.

Suddenly, one of the guys turned to Davin and the conversation turned serious. "Davin, thank you for inviting us over and I think you're right. We may have found our man. Don't you think so Lee?" the guy turned to the guy he had arrived with and asked.

Trek looked up to see them starring at him. "Whoa, hold up. I ain't into no homo crap. I ain't down with that at all!" he said with his hands up as if giving the signal to halt. "Davin, you got something you need to tell me?"

Davin laughed at his childhood friend, while his friends, Lee and Doug, joined in on the laughter. He stood up to go get more drinks for the men. "As a matter-of-fact Trek, there is something I need to tell you. These guys are instructors from Galloping Hill Golf Course and they were looking for another instructor to join them. I know the skills you have in golf, because I've seen them myself. They heard the passion you have when you spoke about the game so they would like you to go out to the club next week for a round of golf with the three of us."

Trek damn near swallowed his tongue when he heard this. "Thank you, kind fellows for the invite, but I don't play golf anymore. I haven't picked up a golf club in six years. He thought back to that awful night six years ago after getting off at the Bell Meadows Country club...

He was walking to his car when a guy he recognized from the club approached him with four other guys he'd never seen.

"Hey, are you the boy they call Trek?"

Trek knew it was about to be trouble, but he had no idea it would completely alter his course of life. The guys beat Trek within an inch of his life that night. Barely breathing, he was left to die while hanging from a tree, bound by his wrists and ankles, where he stayed all through the night. He was discovered the next morning by a group of men out for a round of golf.

Lee was the first to speak out. "Trek, Davin told us about what happened to you, man. He also told us how gifted you are in the sport of golf. We need another strong instructor out there with us to help the young kids entering the world of golf. We're prepared to offer you a fair starting salary with the potential of making up to $150,000 annually, if you have the skills our kids need. Davin seems to think you're a natural at the sport. I'm not going to lie to you, kids of color are skeptical about trusting us, and our goal is to get multiply races of kids interested.

Trek was speechless. Things like this didn't just happen out of the blue, but his love for the game made him want to at least see if the offer was legit. "Let me talk to Davin a little more and get with you guys tomorrow."

Doug had been pretty quiet as he'd listened to the detailed way Trek spoke of the game. He was a tall, muscular guy with red hair, standing a few inches taller than Trek. He was the first to extend his hand out. "I hope to see you next week, man.

We need someone like you over there. You would be the element of surprise for sure," he said as Trek met his hand and gripped it firmly for a shake.

Lee and Doug both gave Davin an awkward dap as they were leaving. "Hopefully, we'll see you next week, Davin, along with Trek," Lee said. "Hey Trek, maybe we can convince this guy to try playing more golf on Saturdays instead of him running on that basketball court," he laughed and said as he closed the door.

Trek looked at Davin when the door closed. "How do you know Lee Dent and Doug Westwood, man? You do know they are two of the best golfers that ever played in the PGA Tours across the country, right?" he added enthusiastically.

Davin just laughed at his friend and shook his head. "I'm aware of who they are, Trek, and I thought it was time for them to know who and what you are. Man, you're wasting away in that project. You were born with a gift, Trek, and it just needs the proper attention to be unwrapped."

Trek scratched his head and rubbed his scraggly sideburn. He hadn't shaved in years and it never bothered him until now. "Davin, do you have an extra razor I can use to clean my face up?"

Davin thought it was a strange question, but he nonetheless went and got one for him to use. "Here's a new razor, man. You can replace it when you start making that big money," he joked. "I have to get back over to the hospital to see about Sheeba. I should be back in about two hours, but make yourself at home. There's food and more beer in the fridge. The remote is on the stand beside the TV." He looked at Trek and noticed the perplexed look on his face. "What's up, Trek?"

Trek leaned back on the couch shaking his head. "Man, when I woke up this morning, I expected my day to go like it has for the last few

73

years. I never saw any of this coming, and I need to bitch-slap myself just to see if I'm dreamin'."

Davin gave a low chuckle while walking towards the door. "Naw, man, you're not dreaming, you're simply about to start living again."

TONYA

Tonya was walking into the deli as two women were about to walk out. She quickly recognized one of the young ladies as her mail carrier who was identical to the young lady who had shot Sheeba earlier in the week, at her place. Her eyes widened in surprise at how different the lady looked out of uniform, quickly remembering the young lady didn't have a uniform on that day either. She just *had* to know why the lady was at her house that day and thank her for saving her life.

"Oh, my God, it's you!" Tonya said while approaching the table occupied by the ladies.

Both, Quanette and Stephine looked at her with no recognition, each one assuming her remark was meant for the other. Tonya looked back to make sure Captain Hunter hadn't arrived before directing her attention towards Quanette.

"Excuse, me but is it possible I can speak with you in private?" she politely asked.

"Do I know you from somewhere?" Quanette asked puzzled.

Tonya looked back, once again making sure the Captain hadn't entered the deli. "Well, I should be asking you the same question," she answered, after she was sure the coast was clear.

Quanette and Stephine looked at each other with total confusion, and by now Quanette was getting perturbed. "What do you mean you should be asking me the same question? You approached me, so apparently, you must *think* you know me."

Tonya looked annoyed, but remained calm. "Can we just have a moment please?"

"Cuz, do you want me to hang around?" Stephine asked Quanette, as she looked at Tonya with raised eyebrows.

"No, Stephine, thanks. You go on home. I know you're tired so I'll call you later."

Tonya and Quanette took a seat in the back of the deli, each one staring at the other suspiciously. "Well, I'm not one to beat around the bush, so let's just cut through the chase... Why did you shoot Sheeba in my house?" She stared directly in Quanette's eyes and didn't blink.

Quanette was totally taken aback and she needed to know what the hell was going on and even more, who was this woman making such a serious accusation against her. "Who are you and what the hell are you talking about?" she asked, looking at Tonya as if she'd suddenly sprouted horns on her head.

Tonya was unmoved and unfazed by her profanity laced attitude. "Look, I know you didn't shoot Sheeba, or "She'bae" as you all call her, just to save me, but it *did* save me. I just needed to thank you for pulling that trigger. If you hadn't shot her, she would have killed me for sure this time around," she replied. Her words were filled with sincere gratitude

By now, Quanette's frame of mind had become jumbled, yet intrigued, and she only knew of only one She'bae. "I have no clue what you're talking about, so would you do me the honor of shedding some light on what it is you're talking about?"

Tonya was becoming aggravated by Quanette's lackluster attitude. "Look, you don't have to pretend with me, I took the fall for shooting Sheeba so you don't have to worry about getting hauled off to jail for it."

Right at that moment, a deep voice interrupted the ladies. "I was right all along. You didn't shoot Mrs. Williams," the voice said.

Recognizing the voice, Tonya turned in her seat and looked up into the eyes of Captain Hunter.

"So…," he began, "is this the young lady you've been protecting?"

Quanette jumped up from her seated position and demanded to know what was going on. "Sir, I don't know what she's talking about, but I have never shot anyone in my life!" "Where were you on the evening of July 12th?

Tonya looked over to Quanette and began shaking her head from side to side. "You are not obligated to answer any questions from the Captain and I suggest you don't answer that question."

"I don't need advice from you and I have nothing to hide. I was on my route at the post office and when it was finished, I went home and was there for the rest of the evening."

"Can you provide witnesses who can attest to what you're saying?" Captain Hunter asked.

Dubiously, Quanette looked at the Captain and then Tonya, wondering what was going on. "Would someone please tell me what the hell is going on here?"

"Ma'am, I'm going to have to ask you to come down to the precinct with me for questioning on the shooting of Sheeba Williams."

"Sir, not to be disrespectful, but I'm not going anywhere with you unless you can tell me what all of this about. I've never done anything against the law in my life."

Tonya saw the sincerity in Quanette's eyes and knew she was telling the truth, so she felt the need to intervene. "Captain Hunter, can't we all please just sit here and talk?"

Alexander Hunter had worked as an Investigative officer for a few years and had been really good, working his way to Captain. He knew Quanette was telling the truth. He also knew Tonya had not been the person who pulled the trigger. "I think that would be a good idea. Before they could get situated, his phone rang, alerting him of an incoming call. He excused himself from the ladies to answer the call in private.

Tonya decided to try and get down to the bottom of what was going on herself. "Are you from the Haynes Project?" she asked the young lady.

Quanette was becoming offended. She'd moved away from that neighborhood to distance herself from it in any way, and now, here was this snooty chick bringing the past back to slap her in the face. But, wait... if she knew about the Haynes Projects, she must have also had ties to the neighborhood herself. It was now Quanette's turn to ask the questions.

"How do you know about the Haynes Project? I remember everyone from there, but I don't recall ever seeing you."

"I lived there for a very short time with my mom and dad until I was attacked by She'bae at the bus stop. I was cut by her because her boyfriend had been talking to me while waiting for the bus."

Quanette covered her mouth as she realized who Tonya was. "OMG, it's you. But you look so different. Everyone thought you'd died because we never saw you again."

"I almost died, but after months of rehabilitation and a number of reconstructive surgeries, I survived that awful day."

"I'm so sorry that happened to you. I witnessed so many girls getting beat down by She'bae because she felt they were a threat to her strange relationship with Davin, but the worst was when she attacked you. So, you obviously had a run in with her again."

"Yes, I did at my apartment. She and Davin are now married, or were married, that is. He and I ran into each other a few days ago. Apparently, she's still obsessed with him because she followed us to my place and attacked me again. She had a gun with her this time. She and I got into a shuffle and the gun was knocked to the floor. She tried to get to the gun, but a girl who looks identical to you come in unnoticed while we were struggling and picked the gun up. She saved my life when she shot Sheeba."

Quanette then realized her twin sister Quanique had to have been the girl Tonya was speaking of.

Captain Hunter returned to the table with a satisfied look on his face. "Well, that was the hospital and they tell me that Mrs. Williams is out of ICU and expected to make a complete recovery. As soon as she's released, we'll have her hauled down to the precinct for interrogation, but until then, Ms. Johnson, your friend and you will need to come down and give me some statements."

Quanette gave a look of disgust at Tonya as she addressed Captain Hunter. "The name is Quanette Hall and there is nothing I can tell you concerning Ms. Johnson. I don't even know her and had never seen her until today."

Tonya looked at the Captain with no emotions as she confirmed what Quanette said. "She's right, Sir. You came in as she and I were talking, but she's not the one you need to question. Even though you've questioned me already, I'll be happy to come back down to the precinct after your interrogation of Mrs. Williams. Just give me a call. If I'm not mistaken, I believe you already have my phone number."

"Yes, I do have your number, Ms. Johnson, and I see no reason why it should be a problem for you to come in after we speak with Mrs. Williams. You ladies have a nice rest of the evening." Captain Hunter stared at Tonya a few seconds longer than intended before offering his hand for a handshake to adjourn the meeting. Finally, he bid the ladies farewell and headed to the door to exit the deli.

Quanette gave a smirk in his direction as he was leaving. "I see you have a fan in the police department. That should work out in your favor. The young lady you saw must have been my twin sister, we are identical. Thank you for not bringing her up into the conversation while he was here.

"No thanks needed," Tonya replied. "If I was going to incriminate her, I would have done that days ago. I think we can work this out, and Ms. She'bae may have worked it out for us by recovering," she stated with a devious grin.

DAVIN

Davin exited the elevator on the seventh floor in deep thought as he was about to pass the nurses' station.

Dorinda was seated behind the desk and saw him approaching. *Damn, what a fine specimen of a man that is right there*, she thought to herself as she eyed him from her peripheral. *How in the hell did he get somebody like that ghetto-ass Sheeba or She'bae or whatever the hell she call herself?* Her thoughts were interrupted when he approached her desk seeking an update on his wife's condition.

"Mr. Williams, your wife has been transferred to the fourth floor. She insisted on leaving the hospital and although she's out of danger, she still has some healing to do. The Doctor had a talk with her and informed her that she's no longer required to remain in the ICU unit. As of now, her current condition doesn't appear to be a threat to her life," Dorinda explained.

Davin forced himself to form a slight smile that displayed his dimples. "Thank you for the update, nurse. I'm not sure if I need to go to the fourth floor and cause a scene like the one that took place earlier. She's my ex-wife, and as you've already witnessed, we're not the best of friends," he admitted honestly. "Nevertheless, if you'd be so kind, please give my number to the nurses' station on that floor should they need to contact me for anything."

He turned to leave, but not before Dorinda took the opportunity to pry on his love life. She'd heard him loud and clear when he referred to Sheeba as his *ex-wife*.

"So, how long have you been divorced, Mr. Williams? I mean, I was given the impression that the two of you were still married. I shouldn't be giving you updates if the two of you aren't together," she probed further.

Davin, however, was far from slow and knew from the start she was attracted to him. So, using her attraction to his advantage, he decided to play along, especially since legally he wasn't entitled to updates on Sheeba. "As strained as it may be, my ex-wife and I still try to maintain a relationship due to our kids. I understand you're not obligated to keep me posted, but I would consider it a *personal* favor if you did." He smiled flirtatiously.

Dorinda gave a wide smile and looked around. "Well, if you just happen to be hanging around here tomorrow about this time, some things may be said that would be of interest to you."

Davin nodded his head up and down taking the hint. "I think that can happen. Maybe, I'll also see you then…" He let the statement linger.

"There's no *maybe* about that Mr. Williams… I'll definitely see you tomorrow." Dorinda was elated, and as soon as Davin was out of site, she did a little two-step behind the nurse's station.

Davin, on the other hand, was disappointed to hear the news of She'bae pulling through. He thought for sure this would be a way to finally get her out of his life, once-and-for-all. He left the hospital and went directly to the spirit store. He figured that he and Trek could at least celebrate Trek's new beginning on life.

TREK

Trek stood in the bathroom staring at his reflection after shaving the straggly beard off. He was so thankful for the second chance he had at a good life. He also reflected on the life he was leaving behind and couldn't believe he had allowed himself to become such a shell of a human being. Then he remembered something his grandmother had said a long time ago: *"God never make mistakes, Trek, He make improvements from what others see as mistakes."* At that very moment, he realized everything he'd gone through was getting him prepared for the life that was now in front of him.

He heard the door open and Davin calling his name. "Trek, where are you man? We have some celebrating to do!" he shouted. "Get on out here!"

When Trek entered the living room, Davin could hardly believe how his old friend looked so fresh. "Man, you should have shaved years ago if that razor got all of that ugly off you like that," he said with a shocked expression. "Man, seriously, you look like the old Trek from back in the day."

Trek gave his chin a rub as he shook his head up and down. "I know man, and I owe it all to you. Davin, man... thank you from the bottom of my heart, dawg. I never dreamed I would have a second chance at the life I was destined to have so many years ago. I promise, man, I won't mess it up this time," he said on the brink of tears.

Davin shook his head from side to side. "Nah, man, you never messed it up. You just had to go through some changes to appreciate it more. It's going to be good from here on out. If you want to thank me, just don't forget a brother when you move uptown."

"Man, you already living uptown. How can I forget my future neighbor?" The guys shared a laugh and a handshake before sitting down on the couch to enjoy the wings and beer Davin had brought home.

Trek dug into the wings and popped a beer open, and then had a thought. "Hey, how is your wife doing?"

Davin looked as if the air had been knocked out of him at the mention of Sheeba. "Sheeba is doing better and she's been transferred to another floor. Maybe you can go with me tomorrow to the hospital."

Trek got choked at the mention of going to the hospital. "Wild horses with a million dollars stuck in their asses couldn't drive me to see that crazy woman."

Davin laughed at Trek's choice of words and shook his head. "I won't be actually going to see her myself, so relax. There's this cute little nurse whose sweet on me and she's going to keep me informed."

"Oh, you got a honey up in there already?"

Davin took a swig from his beer and smugly replied, "Well, she is feeling a brother, but I have my interest elsewhere these days. I figured if you went with me and she laid eyes on you, she'd have a change of heart and go for a real winner."

Trek turned his bottle of beer up before responding. "Psst, I'll take your hand-me-down clothes, food, razors, and right now even your hand-me-down drawers, but I ain't tryna accept your hand-me-down chicks. You don't have the best judgment when it come to the ladies, man. You pull in those crazy wild chics dude."

Davin laughed at Trek's animated description. "Technically, she won't be a hand-me-down, bro. I've never taken her out or even had warm conversations with her. The only reason I agreed to go back to the hospital is to get the inside scoop on Sheeba."

"Who the hell is Sheeba? The new interest?"

Davin snapped his fingers in Trek's face. "Earth to Trek, earth to Trek. Sheeba is that ex-wife of mine, you know her as She'bae. I started using her government name shortly after we married, in hopes she would begin to act a bit more official."

Trek snickered with his fist over his mouth. "How'd that work out for you partner?"

"Go to hell, Trek, you know damn well how it worked out. Moving her ghetto ass out of Haynes only made her ghetto-bougie. My eyes are on Tonya, man, and this time, I'm getting that girl."

Now it was time for Trek to look serious. "Who is Tonya?" With that question, Davin broke out into a full smile and relaxed back into the couch.

"Man, we have a lot of catching up to do, but in short, remember the girl who moved into the neighborhood with her family one summer? Only stayed for a short period of time?"

Trek's memory wasn't that sharp due to alcoholism so he shook his head. "Nah, man. I don't remember much these days."

Davin being persistent in making Trek remember who he was speaking of continued. "Everyone remembers the day She'bae cut the girl at the bus stop because I was talking to her. But we all assumed the girl died from the brutal attack of She'bae."

Recognition set in for Trek at that moment. "Oh yeah, man. That was messed up. She'bae got away with murder for real that day."

Davin shook his head, "Nah, *would* have gotten away with murder had the girl died. Tonya is very much alive and still as beautiful as ever."

Trek looked surprised in more ways than one. "Davin, how do you think She'bae will ever let you be free to date anyone else?"

Davin looked Trek in the eyes as he made his next statement. "Oh, trust me when I say the days of her ruling me are over my friend. That ended with the divorce years ago. I tried treating her like a lady for years, even forcing myself to love her.

It was never appreciated and she never recognized the man I'd become. I thank her for the man I am today, though. Trek, I went to so many therapy sessions because of that woman. She nearly tore my head up, man. I suffer from an illness known as Dissociative Identity Disorder because of her."

Trek looked really confused. "What is Associate Identity what? "It's Dissociative. And simply put, it's having multiple personalities living inside of you. I began to notice it when I started to forget important events and even simple shit like if I'd brushed my teeth in the mornings, or where I parked my car. I began to forget business meetings and damn near lost my job until I went to my primary physician explaining to him my symptoms. He referred me to a therapist."

"What type of symptoms did you have, Davin? I mean we all have messed up memories from time to time. God knows with all of the alcohol I consumed, mine is shot to hell divided in forty ounces."

Davin shook his head in agreement with Trek. "I thought they were normal memory losses for a while. At first I didn't even care, which is another unseen sign. I lacked the desire to do anything. In other words, I was constantly depressed. I would leave work driving home, and end up at the bar, only to forget how I got there. When I'd get home hours later, of course that would lead to Sheeba starting a fight. I will never understand how I never blanked out on her ass and killed her though. The therapist says it's because she was the center of my illness. I learned through many sessions you will shut down when faced with the center of your illness. The center is the root or the beginning, and the very issue that begin your problem.

She'bae was the center of my illness for me. I still have lost moments of my life that I wonder if I will ever get back.

I learned through my treatment, some things are so traumatic your brain will automatically erase it, but part of it always remain with you.

That's when your mental has a shut down, but your body learns to function on autopilot. I learned to accept what my mind refused to release. And once I did, I was able to move on and live a more productive life. I realized worrying about it only caused me more agony and created more negativity in my life. It's a daily struggle for me to beat this illness but with God I am able.

I try to be an inspiration to others, as well and try to encourage them to become more positive. Believe it or not, it's more therapeutic for me to help others have a more positive outlook on life. I think Ms. Tonya would be a little therapeutic for me." Davin smiled with his last statement, but he was very serious. He would never share with Trek about Tonya's condition. He knew it was going to take some zealousness to earn Tonya's trust, and it was a job he was willing to take on because he knew they would be good for one another.

**

As she drove aimlessly listening to music, Tonya replayed her life and some of the most traumatic times she somehow managed to mask behind counterfeit smiles on a daily basis. She thought of the many nights she'd heard her parents screaming and yelling at one another because her father had stayed out all night gambling, often returning home with empty pockets. Of course, staying out all night made it hard for him to go to work the next day which eventually resulted in the loss of his job. Trying hard to maintain the bills and household, her mother began working multiple jobs. She'd leave one job and go to the next, only having time to make short pit-stops at home just to check in on Tonya.

Her dad would always stay home with her till her mom got home for the night, which was always after 10 p.m. then he'd go have a beer with the guys which usually ended up being a brewery fest mixed with gambling of some sort. Her dad was always angry and her mom was never happy, so neither of them ever noticed the taciturn that progressed daily within Tonya.

The day finally came when all her dad's gambling and late-night beer runs destroyed the family, and unfortunately, the place she'd always called home became nothing more than a loveless dwelling place with constant bickering and harsh words.

"What the hell do you mean we're moving, Jon? We're in a good area for Tonya's future! The schools are great and the neighborhood is safe, so why would you want to disrupt that?"

"I'm looking at the future for all of us, Leah. It's either move or be out in the streets where you're never safe. It's gotten too expensive and it's only going to get worse with the little money you bringin' to the table."

"It's my "little money" that has kept us here, Jon. You make triple the money on one job that I make on two, but you choose to gamble and drink

yours away until you eventually lost your job, but I'll get a third job if I have to for Tonya to be in a safe environment. Our child's future should mean as much to you as it does to me."

"Look, I'm moving and you and Tonya can stay here if you think you can handle it by yourself."

"I handle it myself every month anyway with not much help from you, so it won't be much of a difference!"

"Leah, the mortgage is 6 months behind and we have no choice but to move. The house has gone into foreclosure."

Tonya thought of her impromptu visit with Dr. Jain. After the events of what had transpired over the past few days, she explained she needed an emergency visit. After hearing what Tonya had been through, he agreed she needed to come in right away. When her phone rang interrupting her thoughts, her first reaction had been to ignore it, but she suddenly decided to answer.

"Hey, pretty lady, how are you?"

The voice she heard gave her chill bumps. *Does he know what's going on with me right now?* She wondered. *Why did he call out of the blue?*

"Hey, Davin. What's up with you?"

Davin took the phone away from his ear and looked at it as if he'd dialed the wrong number. "I'm sorry, did I catch you at a bad time? You sound preoccupied."

"Nah, you good. What's up?" she asked.

Tonya's voice and disposition seemed to alarm Davin. Then, like a ton of bricks, it hit him— she was different and it wasn't Tonya he was speaking with. It was one of her alters, but he had yet to figure out which one it was. He had to figure it out in order to keep the conversation going in the right direction as the alter that was now in control over Tonya's mind.

"I was wondering if you were busy? I thought I could come over with a movie and we could order a pizza."

"Nah, I don't feel much like having company tonight," she declined.

Davin heard music in the background but didn't recognize the song. I like that beat, who is that you're listening to?" he asked, hoping she'd lighten up.

"Oh, it's a song called *She talks to Angels* by Black Crow."

Is it Mystik? He wondered silently. *I hope not…* He shook his head. *Man, she's a tough one to get to.* He thought as he remembered Mystik all-to-well. He knew something traumatic had to have happened if she had surfaced. "So, what'd you get into today?" he asked.

"The question would be, what did I get out of today, and the answer is jail," she answered. "Oh, my bad, that was yesterday... I think. Oh, hell, who knows when it was."

Shit, this is worse than I thought, Davin told himself, deep in thought. He had to find a way to get on her level so she would let him in.

"Yeah, I have days like that myself so I understand how you feel," he said, sympathetically.

"Then I'm sure you'd understand I don't want to be bothered right now. Thanks for your concern all the same," and with that being said, Mystik gave Davin the dial tone.

***

Trek had a new pep in his step as he walked through the Haynes Project with renewed pride. He was eager to tell his Mom about his newfound freedom and let her know she would soon be escaping the hell hole she called home. He saw Quanette walk up just as he was approaching the stoop and she passed by him nearly knocking him to the ground.

"Excuse me, Sir," She said.

Trek jumped back to see who the strange man was in their neighborhood and even more so, who it was to be getting respect from Quanette like that. However, when he looked back, he didn't see anyone else. Hell, she was always rude to him and everyone else. She'd just called him a low-life, now she was calling him sir? He walked back to see if she was speaking to someone else.

What Trek didn't realize was because of his new attitude, and groomed face, he was different and it displayed with a glow of positivity. Others passed by him looking at him as if he was a total stranger who didn't belong in their neighborhood. In actuality they were right, he not only felt out of place, he was out of place.

He was beginning to feel great about himself once again. Trek walked in the front door and immediately smelled fried chicken like only his mom could cook. His mom came out of the kitchen, ready to give him an earful for coming in smelling like a brewery and looking like a hobo. Surprisingly, her words were caught in her throat as she stared, gazing at her son as if he were a stranger. She dropped to her knees with tears flowing from her eyes and thanked God.

Trek gave her space to praise, he knew how dramatic his mom could be. She was the female version of Fred Sanford, if there ever was a female version. He waited patiently with a watery mouth from the aroma emitting from the kitchen. She rose up from the floor and simply put her arms out for her child to come to her.

***

Quanette knocked on the door as she waited for her aunt to open the door. She looked around the hallway with disgust, grateful she no longer lived there, and even more grateful her children didn't live there. A petite lady with blonde curls answered the door with a look of pure shock on her face. She grabbed Quanette by the hand and carefully looked outside the door past her, and on the sides of the door.

"Child, what in the world is going on? First your sister comes in here in tears talking about some woman dying and she has to hide, now you show up at my door when you have not set foot in these projects since you moved away."

Quanette gave her aunt a big hug. "Hi, Auntie, I don't know what's going on with Quanique. I've tried for so many years to provide the best care for her that I can afford. I thought she was progressing so well, I mean, aside from the fact that she'll never lead a complete life of normalcy. But she seemed to be as close as she could medically get, or so I thought. I ran into a young lady earlier this evening mistaking me for Nique. She was thanking me for saving her life and saying she took the blame for pulling the trigger on She'Bae.

It seems all these years of her getting paid for watching my kids have been nothing more than free checks for her. Apparently, she's been hanging around here in the Haynes Projects while I'm working and the kids have been home alone after school. Auntie, why didn't you warn me that Nique had been making constant trips here during the week?"

Her Aunt released her hug and lead her to the living room where Quanique was sitting in a darkened corner, looking like a scared nine-year-old girl with her knees brought up to her chin. Quanette's heart broke at the sight of her sister and she went over to comfort her.

"Nique, what's wrong sweetie?" Quanette asked as her little sister continued to rock back and forth, as if no one was talking to her.

"Nique, please talk to me baby, I can't help you if you won't let me in. Auntie mentioned someone dying. Was it a friend of yours?" Quanique still did not respond.

Their aunt motioned for Quanette to follow her into another room. "I see Nique over in the projects often, but she never came to visit with me. She was always hanging with those young girls and going to the store for them. I didn't like it because for one, she's much older than them in age, and two, they are cousins to that She'bae girl who used to live here. She has a younger sister who acts just like her, and she and her friends are who Nique is always following these days. That She'bae married that boy she was so crazy over and moved away. Although Nique is the same age as you, she will always have the mind of a child."

Tonya's aunt paused as a thought occurred to her. "Oh, wait a minute, my neighbor did tell me that She'bae and her husband were divorced and she's been spending more time over here. Child, I try not to leave out except very early in the morning and come back home as early as possible, so I really couldn't tell you who's here half the time. I do see Nique coming over but it's usually after the kids have been sent off to school. I must say, I see her leave before school hours are over."

"I never come before the children leave home," Nique interrupted.

Both ladies were shocked that Quanique had quietly come into the room and had been listening to them talk. "I cook breakfast for them every morning and walk them to school, then come hang out here until time for school to let out. Gina is nothing like her sister, She'bae. She doesn't even like her sister because her sister comes around a lot more now and she beats Gina up for no reason. She always makes me leave Gina's house saying I'm a grown woman up to no good, but she's the one who's always up to no-good with Davin. One day after she had beat her sister's ass, I heard her tell her sister she was going to find Davin and beat his ass one last time. Gina was very sad about it so I followed her to stop her. I don't like to see Gina sad," she said solemnly.

And with nothing more to say, Quanique went back to the living room and assumed her position like a little girl with her legs up, face propped down between them, rocking back and forth.

***

Tonya was sitting in her living room drinking a cup of coffee with the TV on mute, computer in hand, while listening to music when she heard her doorbell chime. She got up and looked through the peephole. She took a deep breath before opening the door.

"To what do I owe the pleasure of this visit? I was under the impression I wouldn't be seeing you so soon after this evening."

He invited himself in and took a seat on the couch, cunningly looking around, marveled at what he saw. "Interesting decor you have here, Ms. Johnson," Captain Hunter said as he crossed his legs, getting comfortable.

"Captain, I'm sure you didn't come over to compliment me on my decorum, so how about you give those bushes a break and stop beating them."

"Okay, Tonya..."

"Let's keep this visit formal, the name is Ms. Johnson."

Captain Hunter cleared his throat. "Ms. Johnson, you're right. Unfortunately, this is a formal visit. I have a couple of more questions to ask you concerning where you were this evening after you left the deli."

Tonya had no idea where this line of questioning was coming from, but she did not like where it was going either. "May I ask why the new interrogation Captain Hunter? When we last spoke, Mrs. Williams had made a complete recovery. I'm no Captain of a precinct but nor am I a dummy. When interrogations take a turn, it usually indicates a serious reason."

Captain Hunter looked up at Tonya with an impressive smile. "Funny you should use the word *had* Ms. Johnson. So, would you mind answering my question?"

"I don't think I should be answering any questions without the presence of my attorney, Captain Hunter."

Maybe you would rather come down to the precinct with me and we can compare yours and Mr. Williams' stories of why you both were at Mills Memorial Hospital along the time Mrs. Williams was found unresponsive."

This information didn't seem to faze Tonya at all, in fact her detached response almost surprised the Captain. "It's only been a few hours since you received a call informing you she was on the road to recovery…," she said pausing suspiciously before continuing, "now you tell me she's unresponsive? Which is it Captain? Has she made a recovery or is she finally dead?"

"Ms. Johnson, I'm going to have to insist you come down to the station with me for further questionings. Tonya didn't put a fight, she simply put on more suitable clothing and followed the Captain out the door.

***

Unbeknownst to Tonya, Davin was in another interrogation room being questioned by a detective concerning his whereabouts for the evening. They were both unaware that Quanette and her aunt were on the way in with Quanique to make a confession. They were all unaware that

She'bae had succumb to death by what seemed to be strangulation just a couple of hours prior.

Both Davin and Tonya had been seen by surveillance cameras leaving the hospital around the time Sheeba had been discovered in her hospital bed unresponsive.

EPILOGUE

The young girls listened with intensity as the lady spoke with volume about believing in themselves when no one else does...

"One of the hardest things in life is believing in yourself when, in some way or another, you're ridiculed everyday of your life. Some of you are ridiculed and never even realize it. Most of you are beaten down so much, that it's become a part of your daily living, and the recognition of the great things you do is overlooked by the most important person— that person is you. How many of you, by a show of hands, got up to go to school today?" the lady asked, as she looked from one face to another.

A few hands went up in the air as one girl whispered to a girl sitting next to her, "What's so great about getting up for school? Hell, half of them are flunkin' out before the school year even ends," she said with her face scrunched up.

The lady who'd been speaking heard the rude remark and took it upon herself to elaborate, gracefully answering her own question. "The greatness is most of you have a choice to go to school or not go, because let's face it, your parents are out early for work and sadly some of them are still sleeping from staying out late. Now if I was one of those brave young girls who raised her hands, that one comment made the young lady right over here could have torn me down." Tonya said while pointing in the direction of the young girl who'd made the remark.

What you all must realize is a torn person only knows how to tear other people down; it's the only way they know because they, themselves, are torn in some way and they haven't been re-built. A torn person must keep others torn to make themselves feel as though others are on their level of thinking.

Most of you are here today because you've grown tired of being torn or stuck on one level, yet you don't know how to begin your building process. That's what we show you here at *Build a New You*. My staff and I aren't able to build a new you if you're comfortable with the old you. Unfortunately, I know there are some of you whose only purpose for being here today is to eat some of the good food you smell on the grills. And then, there are those of you who've simply come to be noisy. But despite any of those reasons, today is going to be a great day, because there are some of you who actually came because you're ready to begin a new phase in your life." She looked around, hoping her words would inspire everyone in attendance and not caring if some took offense to her frankness. "We have several booths set up and confidentiality is highly important to us, and it's also an important tool in building a new you."

The same young lady who had been heckling the people for raising their hands decided to take it a step further and heckle the speaker. "I hope you got tools for us to get our grub on," she said sarcastically.

Tonya spoke lowly into a two-way radio, ten seconds later the heckling girl was being escorted out with oohs and ahhhs from the crowd.

Tonya, never breaking her poise began to speak again. "I apologize for the interruptions, but before we begin, is there anyone else not feeling comfortable here, or who may be here for the wrong reasons?"

There was no chatter and a pillow could be heard dropping. This brought about a smile to Tonya's face. She and Gerald decided to start an outreach for the kids in the Haynes Projects as well as neighboring projects.

Captain Gerald Hunter knew there was something special about Tonya the moment he'd lain eyes on her five years prior at his precinct.

When Tonya went in for the emergency visit with Dr. Jain on the day Sheeba had died, she'd finally understood how to integrate her alters.

TONYA'S SESSION

When Tonya left the deli the day she'd run into Quanette, she immediately called her Therapist requesting an emergency meeting. She had been on an emotional rollercoaster that week and knew, without a doubt, she was reaching the end of her rope.

When she'd reached the doctor's office, the receptionist was waiting for her and told her to go on back. She entered Dr. Jains office and he had a pot of coffee waiting for her with her favorite coffee creamer, Coffee Mate Hazelnut. He'd heard the panic in Tonya's voice and knew she would need it.

"Hi, Tonya. I have everything ready for you, just fix your devil's juice and get comfortable," he said with a little humor to attempt to put her at ease. *"You sounded as if you needed something to calm you when I spoke with you on the phone."*

He also had soft, soothing music playing lightly for her in the background. Tonya had been his patient for two years and she would come in weekly, without fail, up until three months ago, when she'd suddenly stopped coming. In those two years, he'd learned a lot about her, including what made her comfortable, and music was at the top of the list for her; it seemed to keep her brain flowing freely. He also knew Tonya had a deeply buried memory of something too horrible for her mind to concept.

She fixed herself a cup of coffee and took a seat as she exhaled deeply. "Dr. Jain, I'm not going to beat around the bush with you. I finally saw Davin and it brought back the very demon I'd struggled with for so long." Dr. Jain didn't say a word. He knew she needed to clear her mind in order for her to co-exist with her alters. "I saw him one day at a market close by my house. I began to have so much hate inside me that I devised a plan to get revenge on him," she told the doctor honestly.

"It began with me luring different men to my home with pretentious interest in them, and to be honest with you, I really don't know what happened after they got there. I would always wake up in my bed with a feeling of confusion. I do know that once I finally saw Davin again, I coaxed him back to my place to exact my revenge," Tonya looked as though recalling the events of this particular night took her mind to another place and time. But, she knew in order to get past it, she had to talk about it, so she continued.

"Well," she said, "things didn't quite go as I'd planned and the situation got totally out of hand." She hesitated and took a drink of her coffee, looking off as if she were trying to find the right words.

"I ended up going to jail this week for a shooting that I was indirectly responsible for, but didn't directly pull the trigger. Davin's girlfriend, She'bae, is the one who attacked me at the bus stop years ago. She followed us back to my house… and-and, the next thing I knew, I-I" she stuttered, "I was in-in a jail cell fighting with another young lady." Tonya's hands began to shake and her body trembled, as the tears welled up in her eyes. "I totally snapped and that's something I've never done before in my life, Dr., at least not that I can recall. I don't even know why I attacked her," she said, unable to stop the tears from falling. "I no longer had control of my actions and all I remember is looking down into her frightened eyes… But even in that state of mind, I didn't like causing someone that type of fear," she told the Dr. admitting her solace kept hidden behind the anger.

This was Dr. Jain's cue to speak. "Tonya, we discussed your illness and you know I'm not sold on the fact that Davin or She'bae is where your illness stems from. You've had a lot to deal with in your life, including your father losing his job and moving your family to a place your mom nor you wanted to live. You nearly lost your life in that very place from the attack against you.

So now, you've been to jail and you had to have felt just as threatened as you had when you were a teenager, but you must remember, it wasn't Davin who nearly took your life," Dr. Jain reminded her. "He was just as much a victim to She'bae as you were.

You went through multiple surgeries and months of rehabilitation which had to be strenuous for you to endure daily, particularly at such a young age. Your mother suffered a mental break-down shortly after you finished your rehab and you had to be responsible for not only her care, but for the care of your ill dad who'd suffered a stroke only a couple of months after you were attacked. When a person experiences many traumatic events, one after the other, the mind has to separate those calamities in order to continue to function. And that's *if* the person is lucky enough to separate the events.

This often times creates a Dissociative Disorder, meaning... you mentally dis-associate your mind from traumatic issues. Your mother wasn't so lucky or rather she didn't receive the proper help like you did with me. It'll always be a constant battle but with the proper care, your mom can fight the battle just as well as you're striving to do. The two of you can, and will, learn to live with an illness that is erasable.

You were doing great in dealing with your illness until you saw the person your mind identified as creating your illness. But wasn't it about four months ago when your mom came home for a visit and you cared for her for a few weeks?" Dr. Jain asked, as she further explained the illness in great depth. "When a patient is faced with the core or what they feel is the core of their illness, it will often cause a switching of the alters. Tonya, I'd like to speak with the other alters with your permission. I may need to use Pentobarbital, an injectable medication used to induce sedation. I'd only need to use a low dosage because I'll only need your mind relaxed enough to allow the other alters to surface and make themselves known."

Tonya didn't speak a word, she only looked at the doctor and sipped her coffee, so he'd continued to explain to her why he felt it crucial to speak with them all. But suddenly, he was interrupted.

"Doc, with all due respect, we don't need any hypnosis to come out. We don't even need Tonya's permission just as Tonya doesn't need our permission."

Hmm, very direct and forward, thought Dr. Jain. *This has to be Mystik.* From earlier sessions, he'd learned that Mystik was the most forward of the alters and usually took the lead role when approached by other people. She was the extroverted personality of Tonya.

"So, Mystik, can you fill me in on what you guys have been up to for the past three months?"

"I'll do the best I can for you, Doc. We've been taking care of Mom which has become a full-time job, in and of itself. Just trying to make her feel loved the way she deserves is almost draining. Doc, this coffee is not getting it for me, do you have some Pepsi cola in here?"

Dr. Jain got up and went over to the mini fridge, pulled out a cold bottle of Pepsi and handed it to her. "I hope it is cold enough for you, Mystik. Is there anything else I can get for you?"

"As I was saying, taking care of Mom while pretending to be strong is harder on Tonya than she even realizes. I take over most of the time when we're at Mom and Dad's house, well Nisey comes out to talk with Daddy because she is, and always will be, Daddy's girl."

"I can speak for myself, Mystik. It's not that I'm Daddy's girl, we're all his girls. And, Tonya, you're always catering to Mom's needs so I show him attention because he needs us as well. He *did* suffer a stroke or did you all forget that important fact?"

"You all act as though you can change the situation but nothing any of us do will ever change what has happened in our lives. The only thing to do is live with it day by day and stop making a mountain out of it."

"Well look who decided to join us today!" Boomed Mystik. "Speaking of mountains, Mystik, what about this Mount Everest you have us all on with your latest rage fits?" Penni broke in.

"I wasn't about to allow She'bae to harm us again, and I sure as hell wasn't about to allow that Big Bertha person to push us around!" Mystik said through an angry voice.

Tonya started to take another sip of her coffee and realized it was a Pepsi. "So, Dr. Jain, how many of them came out?"

Dr. Jain was a world renown Phycologist with many years of experience treating patients with Dissociative Identity Disorder, so to witness the constant switching of Tonya's three alters didn't deter his attention during her session, in fact, it helped him even more. He needed to speak with Mystik first, and hopefully get to the core of the anger within Tonya.

"They all made a brief appearance," he informed her. "How are you feeling right now, Tonya?"

Tonya looked straight ahead as if she were in deep thought. "Dr. Jain, I honestly don't have any feelings right now other than voidance. I feel emotionally drained and incapable of any energy to fight emotionally. I just want to escape from reality. I don't trust myself to make good choices and I don't trust myself to be around other people."

She had such a faraway look in her eyes, like her soul was empty. Dr. Jain knew at this moment that Mystik would take over as Tonya began to shut down.

The room had become so silent, but Dr. Jain knew exactly who to speak to after about two minutes, with no motion coming from Tonya aside from sipping her coffee.

"Mystik, are you here?" Dr. Jain asked.

"Not to be rude, Doctor, but don't you see me sitting here?" Mystik was naturally cynical and never realized how corrosive her words were to others.

"Mystik, do you remember your Dad moving the family out of your first home into the Haynes Projects?" he quizzed her.

"I don't remember moving there," Mystik answered curtly.

Dr. Jain quickly concluded that Mystik wasn't going to be volunteering any information, and knew he would have to slowly pull information out of her until he found out when her existence began.

"Do you remember almost dying while living in the Haynes Projects?" he queried further.

Mystik's facial expression grew satanic as she gazed directly in the doctor's eyes and spat her response. "I have never lived in that dungeon," she said through gritted teeth.

Dr. Jain decided to try a different angle with the evasive Mystik. "Mystik, when is your first memory of coming out to protect Tonya?"

"When she was twelve. One of her dad's drunken friends came to the house on the pretense of visiting her Daddy. He was like an uncle to her, so she thought nothing of allowing him inside the house, after all, he'd visited many times before when her Dad wasn't there. He'd even watched Tonya some days until one of her parents got home. He would sometimes bring her something to eat because he knew she was home alone with no food to eat, a lot due to her Mom working two jobs and her dad hanging out gambling.

Her innocent world became corrupt and her weak mind needed strength. I surfaced on that day, but not before her "uncle" had already mentally raped her of her innocence. I stayed inside hidden after that day. The day she was attacked at the bus stop was so sudden, I never had the chance to come out. I resurfaced again when she was raped by an orderly where she received rehabilitation. It seemed Tonya couldn't get a break in life, it was trauma after trauma. I never left her again after that day. I even carried the baby for nine months as a result of the rape."

This was news to Dr. Jain. Tonya had never brought up a rape, and she most certainly never mentioned having a child. But then he surmised she probably didn't know about the rape. But how could she not know she had a child? He thought almost baffled. He had seen many patients where the host had traumatic things happen to them and they never knew.

"What did you do to him Mystik?"

Karen D. Neal

"I took care of him the same way I did anyone else who harmed Tonya. Most of the time, I can stop them before they harm her. She wouldn't find herself in harm's way if Penni would keep her mouth shut, but she's a part of us and she'll never shut that big mouth of hers up!"

"Is Tonya aware that she was ever raped or carried a child inside of her?" Dr. Jain asked, almost knowingly.

"Of course not! She doesn't know and never will know." Then Mystik leaned forward and almost whispered to Dr. Jain. "You're the doctor here, so you should know I will never allow those memories to process in her brain."

"Mystik, may I speak with Tonya now?"

" I think it's time we end this session for today anyway Doc."

Dr. Jain needed more time but knew better than to start an altercation with this one."

Then as if Tonya had never left the conversation, he heard her say "I don't trust people around me because if they are, I don't know what I might do to them."

Dr. Jain knew Tonya was back, and he addressed her statement as if Mystik had never been there. "Have you hurt people before, Tonya?"

Tonya shook her head up and down with a look of ponderous on her face. I'm pretty sure I have. I mean, there have been times I've found men tied up in my apartment. Some of them have been conscious, some of them not. I only remember seeing them before I blank out, and when I return, everything is back to normal. I did just get released from jail for the shooting of a young lady and I honestly don't know if I pulled the trigger or not. Confidentially speaking, I strongly believe she was shot by someone else, but my life was saved in the process."

Dr. Jain mindfully scrutinized his next statement divulging the information he was about to give. In contrast, over the past two years he knew Tonya had grown in her illness and would be more capable of controlling her alters if she knew the entire truth.

"Tonya, I've spoken with each alter; Nisey, Penni and Mystik. My assessment of Nisey is, she is the little girl within you and has been with you since early childhood. She is the little girl that never grew up and craves attention for love. Penni is brazen and tries things that you would never try as Tonya—she speaks her mind and never thinks of the consequences. She propels you to be different.

That brings us to Mystik... Mystik is the only one who gave me a time of entering your life, and Tonya what I am about to tell you will come as a shock, but you are a strong lady who's endured a lot with trauma after trauma. Mystik informed me that you were raped at the age of twelve by your uncle and then again during your rehabilitation by an orderly.

Mystik surfaced because you were severely traumatized already and your brain refused to accept any more trauma, especially of great magnitudes."

Tonya took in a few deep breaths as her mind processed what she'd just been informed. But her life made so much more sense to her now, the men she'd picked up, the aloofness she often felt, the distrust of people she harbored... It all made sense to her now. Her yearly gynecology exams showed she'd had a pregnancy that she'd denied, because she truly never knew.

Tonya felt like a ton of bricks had been lifted off of her. She felt like she was seeing light for the first time in her life. She'd walked out of Dr. Jain's office that day feeling like a lady in control, and from that day forward she lived her life like she owned it. But she often wondered what happened to the baby she carried.

DAVIN'S SESSION

Davin was the perfect husband in arranging Sheeba's funeral. They shared two children ages ten and twelve, and the loss of their mother was devastating to them. He knew their lives would forever be altered and he wanted to be there for his children every step of the way. He knew in order for him to fully be there for them, he would need additional counseling. Although he'd taken control of his life, She'bae had made it difficult for him and now that she was no longer an issue, he felt an emptiness that was quite bewildering.

When the doctors informed him that She'bae was no longer responsive, he thought the worst was finally over because he'd never have to look over his shoulders again. That should have brought him comfort, but instead it'd brought a grievance he never knew existed. It was on that same day that he decided to call his therapist to schedule an appointment.

Dr. Stanford had treated Davin for many years for Dissociative Identity Disorder and Davin trusted him to find the answer his brain needed in order to completely move on. He called Dr. Stanford on his personal line and requested an unscheduled appointment right away. Over the past two years, Davin and Dr. Stanford had actually become informal associates, and would even participate in recreational fun together from time to time.

"Davin, you have my condolences," Dr. Stanford said as he entered the office.

"Hey Scott, thanks for seeing me so early man," Davin said, greeting the Dr. with a fist pound, as he spoke to him on a more personal level.

"Come go on back and let's get started so we can get you back on the road to healing."

"I really appreciate it," Davin said somberly.

He followed Scott back to his office, a place that he normally felt a sense of comfort. Today, however, he felt like he'd felt on his very first visit, three years prior; full of despair and pessimism.

Scott had coffee waiting for Davin and by the looks of his friend, he was going to need a few cups. Scott had come to know Davin both as a patient and a friend and this morning he would be here for him as both.

"I have some coffee for you Davin. Man, I'm really sorry to hear about Sheeba. I know she had brought you a lot of grief, but she was also the mother of your children, so I can only imagine how you must be feeling."

Davin took a sip of coffee before exhaling and sitting back on the couch. "Scott, I don't even know how I feel myself, man. It seems as if my life is moving in slow motion and there's no fast forward button to propel out of this surreal moment. I mean, when I received the call about

Sheeba being unresponsive, I felt like the weight of the world had been lifted off my body. By the same token, I feel this eerie emptiness inside."

Scott listened, as he watched Davin to be sure he was comfortable relaying his personal feelings to him. He didn't want to rush Davin through this phase and didn't want Davin rushing himself through it either. Shaking his head up and down, he tried to assure Davin that he had his full attention.

Davin scooted up to the edge of the couch and rubbed his face in distress. His eyes displayed a faraway look as he began speaking. "Sheeba brought my life hell, but she somehow turned out to be a damn good mother to our kids. I'm trying to focus on how she was a mother to our kids and the jealous, cruel person she was to me during most of our entire life together. I gotta say Scott, it's causing an internal battle inside of me." Suddenly, he became quiet again and lay back into the couch.

Scott decided to take this opportunity to speak. "Davin, having these feelings are normal when you face a tragedy. Your kids' mother is dead, a woman who has been in your life for fifteen years is no longer here..." Scott grew silent, giving his words a chance to marinate in Davin's mind. "It's just you and me here man, and you can tell me how you honestly feel about Sheeba's death."

Davin sat back up and crossed his right foot over his left thigh. "I'm glad the bitch is finally out of our life."

At the sudden change of attitude, Scott knew who had taken control of the conversation. It was Darrius, the one who didn't have a care for anyone. He knew better than to try and draw Davin back out. He had only met Darrius once, and although Darrius shared a body with Davin, he found Darrius to be extremely obnoxious.

"This punk Davin is making us all look bad with all his freakin' whining! Hell, I feel like shouting, ding dong, the witch is dead, sing it high, sing it low so the entire world can know."

Darrius got up and went to the mini fridge Scott kept in his office. He rudely opened it up, looking inside." Say, man, where do you keep the brewsky around here? This coffee just ain't hitting the spot for me."

Scott remained calm on the outside even though his inside was repulsed at how ignorant this person taking over his friend's body was acting. He cleared his throat and adjusted his tie, the only sign of discomfort he showed.

"Sorry, Darrius, but I don't keep beer inside my office."

Darrius looked back at Scott with a sardonic grin upon his face. "Oh, excuse me, Mr. Doctor, my bad. Just point me in the direction of your coffee pot."

Seeing the pot, he grabbed the cup that Davin had been drinking from and proceeded to pour himself a half cup of coffee before returning to the couch. He reached inside his suit pocket and pulled out a flask then filled the coffee cup with the contents of the flask. Scott remained calm as Darrius filled his cup from the flask. He took a sip from the cup and sat back crossing his right foot over his left thigh with his right arm thrown on top of the couch's back, keeping his left hand wrapped around his coffee.

"So, where were we?" he asked in a matter-of-fact tone of voice. "Oh, yeah, I was saying the witch is dead, gone, caput, and all the above, or rather below," Darrius said, as he looked down at nothing and began to laugh. "Come on, Doc, you know how much grief that woman brought to Davin. Unlike Davin, I don't have mixed feelings about the situation. What I do have is joy, joy, joy, joy, down in my heart!" he sang out sarcastically.

What an asshole, thought Scott. Then, he decided to try and reason with Darrius. "I understand your feelings towards Sheeba, I really do."

Darrius looked at Scott with a frown on his face and asked, "Who the hell is Sheeba?"

Scott realized Darrius never knew Sheeba, he only knew She'bae.

So, he took the initiative to explain to Darrius who Sheeba had been to Davin in hopes that the information wouldn't send Darrius into a spiraling fit.

"Sheeba was the other side of She'bae, and no I'm not saying she has the same disorder as Davin, because I've never met Sheeba and a diagnosis cannot be made on third-hand information, but the She'bae you speak of is a completely different person than who Davin married. Davin had seen the She'bae side of her returning and it was happening more often towards the end of their marriage. Since you seem to have known She'bae quite well, let me introduce you to who Sheeba was according to Davin."

Darrius looked around the office as he patted his pockets and then he turned his attention back to Scott. "Man, I need something stronger than coffee and I need a cigarette, so I need you to hurry this visit along," he snapped rudely.

Scott shook his head in agreement to humor Darrius. "Of course, but I ask that you please listen to details on Sheeba, the wife Davin married and the mother of their two children. She was a quiet person that stayed to herself, and outside of Davin she didn't have any friends.

She drove their kids to school each morning, participated in all of their school activities, and cooked a full course meal every day after picking them up from school. She worked from home as an editor, so her hours were flexible, and according to Davin she built herself to become a powerful voice behind the computer world. She self-taught herself about the job through many online tutorials and by doing countless hours of free work for starving authors, in order to get more training. Within a few years she had also taught herself about graphic design, and her work was in high demand."

As Scott talked to Darrius, he made complete eye contact with him, careful to catch his every reaction from the intricate details he used to describe Sheeba.

Darrius seemed unshakable as he flippantly listened while looking around the room with pretense interest at nothing on the walls, nodding his head ever so slightly with a light chuckle in between.

Nonetheless, Davin's silence was an indication for Scott to continue talking. "Davin's job became more demanding and he began to travel out of town a lot. One day, when he returned home from a two-day trip, he was met at the door with a blunt blow to his head. It was after that when he began having blank spaces in time and would find himself at a bar in the middle of the night— something he wouldn't normally do. Each time he would travel and return home, the rage in Sheeba would be worse than it had been before he'd left, and his memory loss was increasing. He'd awake in strange places with different females which resulted in him going home to his wife, Sheeba, with the scent of different perfumes and other stale odors on him, causing Sheeba's attitude toward him to become more volatile. Eventually, she became a distant Sheeba and a constant She'bae.

That's when he decided to seek professional help, in an effort to encourage her to do the same, but unfortunately, she refused to seek help."

As Scott was looking in Darrius' direction, Darius' head flung backwards, hitting the back of the couch with a force so hard, it nearly made the couch turn over, and blood began leaking from the back of his head. Scott jumped up and rushed over with concern that Darrius had knocked himself senseless. In a way he had, because by the time Scott reached him, he was whining, holding his head with tears in his eyes.

Looking at Scott like a scared child who had gotten in trouble, he began to beg. "Please don't tell my Mommy," he said in a soft childlike tone, "please don't tell my Mommy I got blood on your couch… She's gonna beat me," he cried, "please promise not to tell her, Mr. Scott. I'll clean up the mess I made… Just don't tell my Mommy." His hands trembled revealing his fear and the tears fell from his eyes like huge rain drops.

Scott realized Lil' Davin was now present and terrified of his mother finding blood on the couch. He knew the little boy was between the ages of eight and twelve years of age, so he quickly started reassuring him, letting him know he wouldn't tell his Mother about the blood on the couch.

"Shsss, Shsss, your Mom doesn't have to know anything you don't want her to know." Scott went into the adjoining bathroom and came out with a wet cloth to wipe his head then he cleaned up the small blood spot from the couch. Then pointing to the couch and the wet cloth, he calmly assured Lil' Davin all was fine. "See, the blood is off the couch and you only have a small cut on you, but nothing more than what a scraped knee would be."

This seemed to calm the child inside of Davin as he leaned his head forward onto his lap with relief. When he'd lifted his head back up, he was rubbing his head with a confused look on his face.

"Scott, what the hell, man? My head is throbbing like I just hit a steel wall."

Scott was relieved that Davin was now back and he'd went on to tell him what had transpired. He'd told him about each alter making an appearance and what he thought had prompted the different personalities to surface.

"When you came in you were under so much stress and too weak to control Darrius. While he was present, I introduced him to Sheeba"

This had really confused Davin and he asked how he was able to introduce someone who was dead.

"I introduced him to the type of woman you described to me during your many visits. The introduction must have sent him reeling because he threw his head back on the couch with a hard force and that caused Lil' Davin to make an appearance. At the sight of the blood, Lil' Davin became hysterical with the thought of his mother seeing the blood on the couch and begged me not to tell her. I gathered from his fear, the sight of the blood brought back a childhood memory that in some way involved blood."

Davin looked dumbstruck as he thought of the night he'd seen his mother bleed profusely while her boyfriend beat her. Davin, who'd come in after curfew, had heard her screaming and witnessed the beating. He'd hit the man with a board, drawing lots of blood and shortly that same night, his mom had gone into his and his brothers' room and beat him for missing curfew. He had never shared that story with the doctor turned friend, because it was a painful memory he'd buried deep inside of him. All he'd thought of that night was how he had saved her life and got in trouble for it.

After Davin told Scott of the events that had taken place that night, Scott confirmed to him it could have very well been the childhood trauma that brought little Davin out.

The day he spoke to Scott was the day Davin felt the tension in his body leave. Scott had told him that even though his alters were still present inside him, he'd be able to co-exist with them now that they'd broken through to Lil' Davin.

Darrius had been born on the night his mother beat him for missing curfew, but hadn't surfaced anymore until they'd met She'bae two years later. She'bae had been very possessive of Davin and she'd done some crazy things to draw Darrius out. Over time, it was Davin who ultimately drew Sheeba out to the world. He'd seen the good in her that no one in the Haynes Projects ever saw, because she'd been too busy terrorizing everyone there. Sheeba was never clinically diagnosed because she refused to seek help like Davin had, but he knew he had lived with two very different people.

THE WEDDING

Park Chateau Estate & Garden is nestled midway between Manhattan and Philadelphia on fifteen acres of a beautiful garden and promised as one of the most memorable places to have a wedding. The seventeenth century setting was perfect for the couple's ideal wedding.

As the guest were gathered in the garden waiting for the bride to come join the groom, the live band provided a variety of romantic music. Among the guest were Quanette and Quanique.

Quanette was proud of the progress her twin sister had been making for the past two years. She had finally reached a stage in her treatment where she was allowed to come home and continue treatment through out-patient care. After her confession about shooting Sheeba and careful consideration for her mental state, Quanette had been ordered into a mental institution for two years. After the two years, she would be re-evaluated.

Quanique admitted to shooting She'bae because She'bae made her friend cry all the time and made her feel ashamed around other people and she'd grown tired of it. She was now able to function as an adult after months of counseling and enormous support from her sister and Aunt.

Quanique turned to Quanette and asked, "Why does this place look so old?"

Quanette smiled with pride because her sister allowed her mind to be curious and questioned everything as if she were seeing it for the first time. In a way she was, because Quanique was now seeing them through a young adult's eyes and not through the eyes of the insecure little girl she had been all of her life.

She happily answered any questions her twin asked and never made her feel ashamed about asking them. Quanette had to grow as an adult herself and accept her sister the way she was. She not only accepted her, she embraced her condition with careful arms so her sister would feel as normal as possible.

"The happy couple wanted the wedding to be grand, sort of like Beauty and the Beast." Quanette was explaining further to Quanique about the themed wedding scene that closely resembled the themed movie.

Quanique frowned in confusion and innocently asked, "Does he turn into a beast at night?"

Quanette gave a warm smile at her sister and answered, "No, he doesn't, but the love they have for each other is like that of Beauty and the Beast."

Just then, the wedding march music began to play and everyone immediately got quiet. The groom and best man stood up front with the preacher, each dressed to the nines.

The best man leaned over to the groom and asked, "Are you ready for this life, man?"

The groom had a look of calmness and a demeanor full of confidence. "I have no doubt at all about this day. We're made for each other and no one could ever understand her like I do. I'm ready to take care of every inch of this woman and make her happy everyday of our lives."

The best man smiled and patted the groom on the back. "Here comes your lady now."

The bride had made a special song request to be sang as she walked down the aisle, and as the melody began to play, a young woman began to belt out a beautiful song recorded by Jenifer Hudson titled

Giving Myself.

I never been who I wanted to be

I never felt completely free

Karen D. Neal

No one's ever had all of me

Or made me feel so beautiful and sexy

Now I'm flying like an airplane

Now I'm riding on the open range

Now I'm living out my destiny

I know the truth,

I got it all in you and me

Oh, I'm giving myself over to you

Body and soul

I'm giving it over

I'm giving myself over to you now

Like a brand-new day

Now you and I, we're the face of fame

Karen D. Neal

Ain't nobody got nothing to say, no

And from my feelings

I never have to run away

No more

'Cause he's here

Holding me tight

Every day and night

Oh baby

Can't you see?

I don't wanna be without you anymore

Oh, I'm giving myself over to you

Body and soul

I'm giving it over

Karen D. Neal

I'm giving myself over to you

Oh, I'm giving myself over to you

Body and soul

I'm giving it over

I'm giving myself over to you

For the first time

I can stand in front of someone

Finally

I can be me

I can just let my love spill over

I can cry

I don't have to lie

I can finally let someone all the way inside

She, He, Them: Full Circle
160

Karen D. Neal

All the way

All the way

All the way

Handing myself over to you

Body and soul

I'm giving it over

I'm giving myself over to you

I'm giving myself over to you

Body and soul

I'm giving it over

I'm giving myself over to you

You know it's the right time

I know it's the right night

Karen D. Neal

I know it's the right life

I know you're the right man

I know I'm the right girl

Come on now feel it

You feel it?

I'm ready to give it over to you

Body and soul

I'm giving it over (I'm giving it over)

I'm giving myself over to you now

All the way

All the way

I've never loved nobody else…"

Tonya walked up the manicured garden's path alone in a custom design nude wedding gown covered with peek-a-boo lace, and a veil that flowed from her head to her feet in a perfect circle. She looked over to her right ever so slightly catching a glimpse of her guests.

Among them she saw Dr. Jain and smiled with relief that he'd been able to make the hour and half drive to be at her wedding. She'd been integrated with her alters for the past year, but felt even more reassured knowing her therapist was only a few feet from her as she walked down the aisle to her groom.

Her father sat in a wheelchair up front with her mother and their nurse. Tonya looked over at them and her Mom had tears rolling down her cheeks.

Her dad was partially paralyzed after suffering a stroke while Tonya had been in rehabilitation as a teenager. She looked ahead to her groom who had the biggest smile on his handsome face, starring at his wife to be.

She took a quick glance to her left and saw just as many people on that side as she'd seen to the right of her.

This was the happiest day, ever, of Tonya's life, because she had allowed her heart to freely feel love without fear of disappointment.

***

As he watched Tonya walk down the aisle, Davin gave her a reassuring smile and mouthed, "You got this." He wasn't so sure if he had it though. He had convinced himself that this day would be a breeze and anyone looking at him would think it was a breeze for him as he looked out at the crowd, searching for the face he needed to see.

Scott Stanford looked up front at his patient turned friend and mouthed to him. "You got this." Davin smiled with a little more relief just knowing his therapist/friend, Scott was out in the crowd should he need him.

"Who gives this woman's hand in marriage?" the preacher asked.

Although Tonya's dad was not physically able to walk her down the aisle, Tonya still wanted him to be a part of her special day. The nurse pushed her dad forward in the wheel chair as he said, "I do," then he looked at his daughter and her groom and said, "take care of my daughter."

Captain Gerald Hunter looked at his soon to be father-in-law with a big smile and said, "I will, Sir, every day of our lives."

Tonya wanted them to write their own vows, no matter how simple, as long as it was from the heart. Gerald was becoming nervous looking over at Tonya.

She gave him a reassuring smile and mouthed, "You got this."

He smiled back at her and mouthed, "We've got this."

After they said their vows, the preacher looked into the crowd and said, "I present to you all, Mr. and Mrs. Gerald Alexander Hunter!"

Gerald kissed his bride long and hard. He looked over at Davin. "Thanks for being my best man, I know it was Tonya's idea and you were her friend originally, but over the course of the year, you've become like a brother to me, man. Through you, I have learned a lot about the illness you and Tonya share.

Davin, man, I'm so grateful to you, please know that *we,* are here for you anytime you need us."

Davin gave Gerald dap and said, "Just take care of her, man. Make sure she's happy every day of her life. She's been through a lot over the years and now it's time for her to get the happiness she deserves.

As they say in our group therapy, you got this…"

NATIONAL HILLS AUGUSTA, GA

Trek became an instructor at the prestigious Galloping Hills golf course, after participating in a few rounds of golf with Lee, Doug, and occasionally Davin, who later convinced him to try out for web.com golf.

It was a vigorous year for Trek, but he·was determined to become a success in the sport for which he had a love and a rare talent. He participated in over thirty tournaments throughout the states, placing in the top fifteen, winning twelve, and securing himself an invitation to the PGA US Open Tours.

He was grateful for the day Davin came into the neighborhood and saved him from himself. He was able to move his Mom out of the Haynes Projects and into a middle-class neighborhood. He was even able to employ a couple of his friends who proved to want a change as well. He was a prime example of not becoming a product of your environment— he had learned if you stumble, catch your balance and try again.

Trek was now a professional golfer, and today he was standing on the prestigious greens of the Augusta National, along with some renowned professional golfers. He had Davin as his caddie for the event, and his Mom was there to witness her son play on the well-known Masters Tour. No one was prouder than she was on this day.

Tonya and Gerald had even flown down and secured tickets for the beautiful Sunday.

Trek saw Dorinda who had Davin's children, along with her daughter who was the same age as Davin's daughter dressed in shorts and hats. Perfect clothing for the hot weather in Augusta Ga so early in the year. Aprils in Georgia were unpredictable when it came to the weather you never knew what each day would bring.

Davin began dating Dorinda a year earlier and they had become quite the couple. He, along with

Davin, felt Dorinda had been placed in Davin's life by God, because they seemed so perfect for one another, if *perfect* existed.

As they walked to the 18th hole, the crowd followed while applauding the players who had made it this far. Trek's dream had been to play in the Masters, but he'd never thought he'd be where he was at this moment. Along with two other players, he trailed Dustin Johnson with only two holes to play. Trek had birded the last two holes giving him a chance of a lifetime and making history as a Masters' winner.

The magnificent evening was calling to the crowd and the heat was molten. Dustin Johnson was leading by 5 strokes with a score of -9 when he last saw the board. He had no idea the bonfire unfolding behind him.

Dustin birded the last hole with the confidence that his -10 would secure him the famous Green Jacket, but upon walking into the clubhouse, he was met with strange looks from everyone inside.

He went over to get some water, when one of the men condescendingly said to him while pointing to the TV monitor on the wall, "I guess Trek Patterson is one determined player. He played some amazing golf this evening in order to catch up with you on the leader board."

Dustin Johnson looked up on the monitor and felt a sudden sickening feeling in the pit of his stomach. Trek Patterson had -10 and if he birded this hole, he would win the tournament. "Got dammit, this cannot be happening to me when I was so close to finally winning a Green Jacket!" Dustin spat.

He ran out of the clubhouse back onto the 18th hole, hoping to have a tie-off with the new guy. However, the guy had driven the ball 448 feet in only 2 shots and was now in putting range on the par 4 hole with only 18 feet standing between him and the Green Jacket.

The crowd became so quiet, the chirping of the birds was the only sound that could be heard.

The commentators were in awe as they too witnessed the turning event of this game. Not since the Greg Norman and Nick Faldo fiasco had they seen anything like it.

Trek should have been nervous but he was far from it. He looked over at his wife and smiled. Quanette looked back at him holding their little girl, Chloe, in her arms. She pointed at Trek and smiled as she mouthed, "You got this…"

Dorinda saw this exchange between Trek and Quanette and she smiled too knowing she had done the right thing in getting rid of Sheeba.

On the evening of Sheeba's death, she'd received a beautiful, large bouquet of flowers that were a mixture of lavender and white blooms.

Sheeba had been so excited convincing herself Davin had sent them, she didn't know the flowers were a mixture of Hemlock and Aconite. Aconites come from a plant known as wolfbane, which is so toxic, if a person touches them, the poison will absorb into their integumentary system causing a very quick death. *She had smelled them all day, with happiness that Davin was coming back to her.*

Dorinda walked into her room later that day and noticed Sheeba barely breathing. She'd put some rubber gloves on and carefully taken the bouquet of flowers out of the room to get rid of them. Sheeba died of asphyxia from the flowers and not at the hands of anyone. Dorinda would never tell a soul what she did that day, not even the love of her life.

"And it goes in! Unbelievable! Trek Patterson has won the 2018 Green Jacket!" the commentator yelled out in excitement.

The crowd went wild as everyone rushed onto the green to congratulate Trek on his win.

He went over to Davin with tears in his eyes, "Man, thank you for caddying for me this week. I could feel this win, man, and I wanted you beside me when I won because you are the reason I'm here today."

Davin was so proud of Trek, he gave him a bear hug with tears of his own he said, "Nah, I can't take this credit, man. You wanted this and you went for it with everything you had."

Davin looked around the green and pointed as he said, "You did this my friend! You got this!"

WORDS FROM THE AUTHOR

Mental illness lives among us daily, whether it be on the inside of us or living within our loved ones. Prevalence of mental disorders has been studied around the world with provisions of studies on how common it is for the illness to affect one out of every four people.

When you hear the word *mental*, the uneducated mind will automatically think crazy, but if you did a study or research, you'd be surprised what falls in the category of mental illness.

Among the category, but not limited are:

Dissociative Identity Disorder: The symptoms of a dissociative disorder usually first develop as a response to a traumatic event, such as abuse or military combat, to keep those memories under control.

Anxiety: which have several categories within itself may be the leading mental illness in the world. The following is a list of the types of anxiety:

Panic Disorder: Feelings of terror that strike suddenly and rapaciously with no warning or the individual may experience sweating and chest pain that could feel like a choking.

Social Anxiety: Feeling uncomfortable around other people; specific phobias where a person has a fear of a specific thing, and lastly you have generalized anxiety where the person has excessive unrealistic worry and tension for no known reason.

Bipolar Disorder, Depression, Eating Disorder, Schizophrenia, Substance Abuse

Educate yourself on these disorders and if you, or someone you know, are experiencing some of the symptoms, get to a doctor for help. This is not an illness that you can self-diagnose, and you could make a situation worse if you attempt to self-diagnose.

The following links are cites with opinions and real studies on mental illnesses.

https://en.wikipedia.org/wiki/Prevalence_of_mental_disorders

https://www.nami.org/Learn-More/Mental-Health-Conditions/Dissociative-Disorders

Karen D. Neal

Author/Publisher Karen D. Neal

Contact Information

Facebook:
https://www.facebook.com/KARENDNEAL

Google+:
https://www.google.com/?gws_rd=ssl#q=kar
en+d.+neal

Instagram: @karen_d.neal

LinkedIn: Karen D. Neal

https://www.yagirlkarend.com/